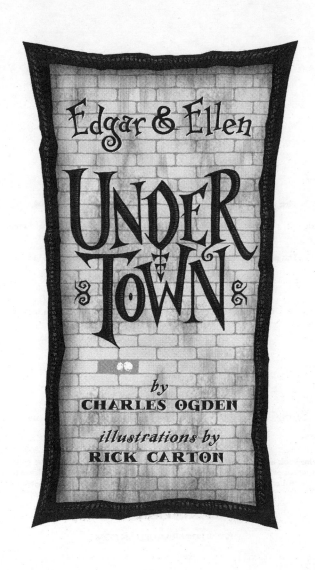

Edgar & Ellen

UNDER TOWN

by
CHARLES OGDEN

illustrations by
RICK CARTON

SIMON AND SCHUSTER

Watch out for Edgar & Ellen in:

Rare Beasts
Tourist Trap

First published in Great Britain by Simon & Schuster UK Ltd, 2004,
A CBS company
Originally published in 2004 by Tricycle Press, a little division of Ten Speed Press,
P.O. Box 7123, Berkeley, California 94707.

This paperback edition published in 2008 by Simon & Schuster UK Ltd.

Design by Star Farm Productions LLC.
Text and copyright © 2004 by Star Farm Productions LLC.

1 3 5 7 9 10 8 6 4 2

Simon & Schuster UK Ltd
1st Floor
222 Gray's Inn Road
London WC1X 8HB

A CIP catalogue record for this book is available from the British Library.

ISBN: 978-1-84738-322-8

Printed and bound in Great Britain by
CPI Cox & Wyman, Reading, RG1 8EX

WWW.EDGARANDELLEN.COM

HERE IS MY DEDICATION—

To *Jen,*
Whose pen put colours down,
Who made me bricks of red and brown.
For shining light on paths below
I owe my end to *Popio.*
To *Chris,*
For brewing fragrant spices,
David for his singing vices,
The Farm, who moved me in a crisis
To soil where richer kernels grow.

—CHARLES

DEEP BELOW, IN DARKEST STRAITS...

Morning Breaks

The rising sun lingered behind the eastern hills of Nod's Limbs, reluctant, perhaps, to show its face on such a crisp morning. Municipal street sweepers Claudius Roe and his son Charlie neared the end of their morning rounds and paused at the foot of a driveway. Leaning on his broom, Claudius read the front-page headline of the day's *Gazette:*

KNIGHTLORIAN HOTEL CONSTRUCTION TO BEGIN

Smelterburg Construction Corporation Racing
to Meet Foundation Day Deadline

"So, they're building that hotel after all. It's a miracle considering the French Toast Festival disaster – all those traumatised celebrities," he said.

"That journalist gal didn't seem to mind," said Charlie. "Thanks to her article on our town, the mayor gets to build his hotel, and we get tourists to sweep up after—"

His father jerked his head around.

"Pop? Hey, Pop, are you okay?"

Twigs snapped and a low snarl rose from the cemetery across the street. Charlie could see faint outlines of gravestones, row upon row, solemn and still in the dim morning light. The sound persisted as something flitted among the stone markers and disappeared.

The snarl stopped and all was silent.

"Uh, Pop? It, uh…it's almost dawn…. Maybe we'd better, uh…move along…."

Charlie turned to see his father swiftly walking away.

"When you're right, you're right," Claudius called back.

As the two men hurried off, a hooded figure passed from the cemetery into the neighbouring junkyard, stopping to gaze at a very tall, very narrow house. One light shone through a round window on a top floor; the rest lay in darkness.

A hand reached into the folds of a cloak and withdrew a dingy photograph. It revealed a bizarre scene of dozens of terrified people, coated in goop and shrinking in terror beneath a cloud of attacking birds. In the background, however, there were two figures dressed in striped footie pajamas who did not cower. They looked nearly identical but that one was a girl and the other a boy. In the midst of chaos, they appeared to be dancing.

The figure crumpled the photograph, stashed it inside the cloak, then vanished into the mist.

1. Pie for Breakfast

Nod's Limbs was abuzz with news of the luxury hotel. The mayor planned to build it on the site of the town's junkyard, replacing "that civic eyesore" with "a monument to culture and sophistication". Soon the Knightlorian Hotel would be more famous than the Nod's Limbs clock tower, the Crabby Apple Tree, and the seven covered bridges spanning the Running River.

Construction was nearly underway and only a few days remained until Foundation Day, the hotel's official kick-off celebration when the cement foundation would be poured.

At the breakfast counter of Buffy's Muffins, local business executive Marvin Matterhorn stabbed his fork into a wedge of chocolate chip pie.

"A luxury hotel is the best thing for us," he said. "Brings in the money, tourism does."

The other customers at the counter nodded their heads.

"True, true – but I do feel sorry for Mr and Mrs Elines," said Buffy, pouring coffee for a pair of elderly ladies. "They've run the Hotel Motel for forty years, and now they may have to shut down."

"Nonsense," said Marvin Matterhorn. He pointed a forkful of pie at Buffy. "Competition is good for business. Makes you tough! Take this development firm from Smelterburg, for instance—"

"Oh, don't get me started on them," interrupted Buffy. "Out-of-towners. Why couldn't Mayor Knightleigh hire good old Smithy & Sons? Local builders for local buildings, I say."

"Wrong again," said Marvin Matterhorn. "The Smelterburg Construction Corporation is famous for quick work. Speed equals time and time equals money! Mark my words, Buffy: the sooner that hotel opens, the sooner you'll make a fortune feeding your amazing chocolate chip pie to tourists."

With that, he popped the fork into his mouth and chewed for a moment.

His cheeks welled up like a frog's. He sputtered and coughed and spat out hunks of pie. Buffy and her other customers looked on, wide-eyed.

"THOSE – AREN'T – CHOCOLATE – CHIPS!" bellowed Marvin Matterhorn. He peered at a black chunk on his plate. "This looks like… like… *shredded tyre!*"

Buffy opened a ceramic jar marked "CHIPS" and scooped up a handful of the contents.

"Someone replaced my gourmet morsels with little bits of rubber!" she exclaimed. "Who did this? Why? Only a truly terrible person would do such a thing."

She was half right.

2. Bad Eggs

There were *two* terrible persons in Nod's Limbs capable of corrupting pie in such a way. They were twins, a brother and a sister, and they lived alone next to the cemetery on the outskirts of town. They were tall for their age, scrawny and pale, had black hair, and always wore the same matching pairs of striped footie pyjamas. Years ago their parents had departed on an around-the-world vacation, according to the note they'd left behind, and they had never returned.

The twins' house was a muddle of greys from bottom to top, towering eleven narrow storeys above ground and sinking two floors below. Over the front door was carved the word *schadenfreude,* which means "pleasure derived from the misery of others".

The two inhabitants of this house kept odd habits and practised odder hobbies, and any time they spent to themselves gave their fellow citizens welcome peace. The twins neither read the local paper nor did they participate in town gossip – and so it was that they knew nothing of the hotel moving in right next door.

3. Flung

Twanggg!

A small, greasy hairball flew straight up into the air and landed like a wig on Edgar's head.

"That's a good style for you, Brother," snickered Ellen. "With long hair, you look like the ugly version of me."

"You *are* the ugly version of you," Edgar retorted. He yanked the shaggy animal from his head and

pitched it at his sister. Ellen caught Pet in mid-air; its single yellow eye bulged, but the creature didn't resist as Ellen shoved it back into the catapult basket.

For weeks, the twins had been in the Black Tree Forest Preserve, building – or, more precisely, failing to build – their latest contraption. A series of obstacles continued to thwart them. Only the night before, the twins had sneaked into the Nod's Limbs Grammar School playground intending to swipe the giant tyre swings to use as wheels for the catapult. But Principal Mulberry, having received several reports of dizziness from wildly spinning children, had removed the tyres, shredded them, and scattered them as padding under the slide. ("A dizzy child is not a learning child," she had said at the time.)

"Don't get rude with *me*, Edgar," said Ellen. "I'm not the one who tightened the springs until they snapped."

"You brought me springs that were too short. This catapult couldn't fling Pet a foot, and it's all—"

"—your fault."

"—*your* fault."

Ellen charged Edgar, who swiftly hopped aside. But as she flew past, Ellen gripped her twin's collar, pulling him with her into the bramble. They wrestled out of the brush and across the forest floor, jabbing and kicking with their gangly limbs. Frightened woodland creatures scampered away from the tumble-weed of black hair and striped pyjamas.

Finally exhausted, Ellen leaned against a mossy log, panting. "Why is it so hard to build a simple catapult?"

Edgar spat out a mouthful of pine needles. "Because nothing about a catapult is simple."

4. Back to the Drawing Board

"Just one more trip to the Gadget Graveyard," said Edgar, "and I'll show you what a proper spring looks like." He removed a small tape recorder from his satchel and spoke into it: "Observation #326: don't leave Ellen in charge of finding parts."

Normally, the thought of going to the junkyard next to their house made Ellen quite happy. She and her brother always found objects there that they could use in their schemes – birdcages, grindstones, mannequins, stuffed swordfish, industrial cotton candy spinners. Once Ellen recovered a stack of rusty stop signs and placed them every twenty feet down Cairo Avenue, the busiest street in town. This caused a traffic tangle of proportions never before seen in Nod's Limbs, and many commuters, unaccustomed to navigating such chaos, lost a whole day's work in the jam.

Today, however, after dozens of trips to the Gadget Graveyard looking for catapult parts, Ellen groaned at the thought of more scavenging. Worse still, they had seen Heimertz roaming the garden earlier.

For as long as the twins could recall, Heimertz had been the caretaker of their house and grounds, though his caretaking activities usually consisted of seemingly useless tasks such as peeling bark from dead trees and watering rocks. The twins never heard him speak a word, yet he always seemed to know what they were up to. His unpredictable behaviour and broad, unwavering smile instilled in Edgar and Ellen the only sense of mortal dread they'd ever felt.

That very morning, when they'd passed his ramshackle shed, they had heard his eerie accordion music. Even as he played the wheezing instrument, Heimertz had stood at his cracked window, gazing at them.

Ellen shuddered at the memory.

"Cheer up, Ellen," said Edgar. "Imagine the day we get the catapult operating. We'll steal the new zoo displays from the wax museum and fling them into the playground at break. Pigs will fly. And cows, and chickens…"

"Okay, okay," said his sister with a sigh. "But if we get it working, I want to toss termite nests at Stephanie Knightleigh's new tree house."

She rubbed her little finger, which had no nail. She had lost it in a clash with the mayor's daughter.

Edgar clicked the tape recorder on again. "Observation #327: Ellen has severe grudge problems."

5. Bricks and Stones May Break Your Bones

Edgar and Ellen weren't the only ones with business in the Gadget Graveyard. Near the entrance, they noticed a pile of bricks as high as their pointy chins and as wide as their outstretched arms. Next to the pile sat several bags of mortar mix.

"Look at all those bricks!" exclaimed Ellen.

"Only a fool – or a Nod's Limbsian – would throw away material like this," Edgar replied. "You know, Sister, we should focus on something besides the catapult for a day or so."

"What are you thinking, Brother?"

"Well, we do owe Principal Mulberry for destroying our tyres." He pulled a meat pounder from his ever-handy satchel. "What if we smash up all these bricks and spread the pulverised pieces on the playground? That will make for some nice bloody knees."

Ellen grabbed the meat pounder from her brother and hit one of the bricks. A tiny flake chipped off.

"It would take twenty years to smash them all. I think I prefer something more immediate. Let's pour the mortar mix into the school swimming pool."

"That trick didn't work with oatmeal, remember?" Edgar paused. "Aha! What are bricks normally used for?"

"Breaking windows. No – sinking toy sailboats."

"I mean, what do other people do with bricks?"

"Build things, I suppose. Edgar, I refuse to work on that battering ram of yours again."

"That was a trivial plan. This is *tremendous,*" Edgar said. "We're going to brick up the door to the school. And maybe the windows too, if we have any mortar left over."

Ellen tugged one of her pigtails.

"Not bad," she said. "This new plan sounds more fun than that wretched catapult. But how can we move the bricks?"

"We'll drag them on that car hood we use for sledding."

"Hauling tons of bricks across town would only invite unwelcome questions."

"*If* we travel above ground, Sister," said Edgar, "but not if we go below."

6. What Runs Beneath

The unlikely placement of the Nod's Limbs Cemetery directly beside the junkyard was the inspiration of Nod's Limbs' first mayor, Thaddeus Knightleigh, who decided to gather all the unpleasant features of town in a single, out-of-the-way location.

Amid the cemetery's traditional headstones and grave markers stood one of the grandest mausoleums in three counties, the final resting place of Thaddeus and the long line of Knightleighs who had served as mayor ever since. At the foot of this ornate marble tomb, a storm drain served as the twins' gateway in and out of the sewers.

In most towns, sewers are dark, dirty, and smelly. No one goes into them unless they absolutely have to – or unless someone pushes them. Most Nod's Limbsians had not ventured into their sewers either, but if they had, they might have been surprised.

The sewers of Nod's Limbs were a marvel of engineering and architecture. When they were first built centuries ago, they were almost as cheery, bright, and clean as the streets they flowed beneath. Silas Smithy, the master builder who erected all the earliest structures in town, intended the Nod's Limbs sewer system to be his greatest work: a series of beautiful underground boulevards where one could enjoy a riverside stroll in even the foulest of weather. Evenly spaced grates allowed sunbeams to pierce the darkness, fully lighting the wide limestone walkways below. Stone arches held the vaulted ceilings aloft and gargoyles and decorative carvings gave the sewers the look of a medieval abbey.

But the most remarkable element of the sewers was their canals. Flowing alongside the walkways were streams of rainwater collected from gutters and drains around town. These canals ran through the middle of the tunnels and, in fact, carried no sewage. Wastewater (the nasty stuff collected from toilets and sink drains) flowed through pipes directly beneath the waterways. Occasionally, in the early days, the odd leaf or twig (or the very odd piece of litter) found its way into the canals, but for the most part the sewers had remained free of unpleasant smells and dirt.

These grand boulevards ran directly beneath every street in town. Even the newer neighbourhoods had wide tunnels below them, though these modern additions could not compare with the sophistication of the originals.

When Nod's Limbs was just a young town, its maintenance department dutifully scoured the sewers once a week, so that the white stone gleamed and the waterways sparkled. At the time, Silas Smithy dubbed it "the greatest architecture *beneath* the face of the earth."

Alas, it was a doomed idea. Maybe because the cost of cleaning the streets and public buildings rose as the town grew or maybe because only the Smithy family ever fully embraced the notion of a pleasurable walk underground, but as time passed, sewer cleanliness dropped off the list of civic priorities. The town paved over many of the grates, leaving the sewer system cold and dark. Grime soon found its way into every crevice and crack in the limestone. Dark stains were left to spread over the walkways, up the walls, and across the high archways. Unless one looked carefully with a strong flashlight, it was difficult to see anything of the craftsmanship of sewers built to evoke the finest promenades of old Europe.

7. Pilferer's Progress

Edgar and Ellen began exploring underground when they were quite young, and they knew the twisting paths beneath Nod's Limbs as well as most people know the route to the bathroom in the middle of the night.

That evening, the twins wound through the sewers, hauling load after load of bricks to the manhole directly beside their school. The going was slow: the pathways were damp and slippery, and the only light to guide them came from Edgar's headlamp. More than once their cargo almost slid into the canal, which had been overrun long ago by muck and teeming organisms that preferred life in the dark and the wet.

Finally, with the last brick stowed, Edgar sat atop the pile and pulled a set of drawings from his satchel.

"Tomorrow night, we brick," he said, spreading the plans across his lap. "A wall five layers deep will take them a while to dismantle — at least a week, I'd say."

"At least," agreed Ellen.

"We'll start moving the
bricks when it gets dark so we
can begin as soon as Janitor
Clunch finishes his rounds," Edgar said.
"I secured a pulley to the rim of the manhole to hoist them. You have the bucket?"

"For the hundredth time, yes," said
Ellen.

"We cannot afford to overlook
anything, Ellen," said Edgar. He rolled
up the sketches and placed them in
the bucket. "I want to give Nod's
Limbs Grammar our best effort."

"Let's see Principal Mulberry
try to shred *this*," cackled Ellen.

Despite the aches in their
backs and arms from a day
of heavy lifting, the twins
skipped home through
the sewers and
sang:

To our principal's chagrin,
The day's delays will soon begin.
We'll show the school the wile of twins
When brick by brick, we brick it in!
Tripping through the smelly sewers
Where the faint of heart demur,
Dark and damp and dirt endure—
Perfect paths for trouble brewers.
Down underground where filth abounds,
We're right at home when under town!

8. Hitting the Wall

As Edgar and Ellen headed to school the next morning, they saw cars backed up Cairo Avenue all the way to Ricketts Road. Traffic – whether cycle, scooter, or station wagon – stood still. Motorists honked horns and wailed.

"When did you put the stop signs out again?" asked Edgar.

"I didn't," said Ellen. "This must be *your* work – you pulled one of our pranks without me!"

"*I* had nothing to do with this," said Edgar.

They couldn't see the reason for the traffic jam until they neared Nod's Limbs Grammar.

A cluster of teachers, parents, and kids stood on the school lawn, apparently in no hurry to get inside despite the chime of the late bell. The loiterers all faced the covered bridge across the street, where drivers shook fists in the air or shouted in frustration.

The twins pushed to the front of the crowd, and there they saw it: a brick wall entirely sealed the entrance to the bridge.

An equally long line of vehicles waited on the other side of the river, where a large dump truck furiously blew its horn.

"This is exactly our idea," said Ellen, "except instead of the school, it's the bridge!"

"It's like someone copied our plan, Sister. But who? Who knew what we were up to?"

As if in response, sunlight pierced the clouds. The wall had seemed flat and even, but now shadows indicated that this was not so: some bricks stuck out from the rest of the wall. Those standing nearest, including the twins, gasped as they realized that this was no random pattern of poorly placed bricks. Rather, they spelled a name: "THE MASON."

9. Rest Easy, Ye Fearful Citizens

An alarmed murmur rippled through the crowd. Whispers of "What kind of monster is this Mason?" and "Why would anyone obstruct an innocent public thoroughfare?" and "Jeepers!" passed from one concerned citizen to another. The arrival of a very important automobile, however, cut the outcry short.

The mayoral limousine rolled down the sidewalk and parked in front of the bridge. Mayor Knightleigh stepped out of the car, strode up to the wall, gazed at it briefly, then turned to face his townspeople.

Up front, Penny Pickens whimpered and hid in her mother's skirts. Behind them, Marvin Matterhorn bemoaned the dangers of rebels causing delays to work. Mrs Elines clutched her handbag and nervously looked about. Mayor Knightleigh cleared his throat.

"Ladies and gentlemen, children of Nod's Limbs: Please, do not panic! I have arrived, and everything is under control. I, Mayor Knightleigh, pledge to find this Mason and have him arrested. May he live out his days in the confines of a jail cell, for I do not negotiate with vandals!"

The mayor paused. Several people still looked doubtfully at the Mason's frightful handiwork.

"What do we do, Mr Mayor? We must protect our children!" called out Miss Croquet, a local school-teacher.

"Of course, my dear. Until this villain is apprehended, I am imposing a curfew of 6pm or sunset, whichever comes first. Please be in your houses by this time, and remember to lock your doors. We do not know the nature of this Mason, but we must consider him alarming and dangerous."

Parents nodded solemnly and ushered their children away from the crime scene.

The mayor turned to the drivers in their cars. "To all of you dutifully on your way to your places of employment: Do not let this slight setback impede your speedy arrival. After all, we do have *six other bridges* in this wonderful town. Let us be thankful that my great-great-great-great-great-great-great-grand-father Thaddeus had the foresight to build them! Even so many years ago, he knew a day like this might come."

10. What Yumley Saw

"Gone. All of it gone," said Ellen.

While everyone listened to Mayor Knightleigh's speech, the twins descended into the sewers to the spot where they had dumped their bricks mere hours earlier.

There were no bricks, nor mortar, nor plans to be seen.

"Robbery!" said Edgar. "Robbery most foul!"

"I can't *believe* you left that diagram here for anyone to take," said Ellen. "Why didn't you string up blinking lights and hang a big sign while you were at it: 'DIABOLICAL MASTER PLANS HERE; GET 'EM WHILE THEY'RE HOT'?"

"This is shameful criminal behaviour," fumed Edgar. "Where was the Nod's Limbs Police Department when this troublemaker was afoot?"

"Brother, it seems we're no longer the only ones using these sewers. The Mason stumbled on our supplies easily enough, but maybe he didn't make a clean getaway."

Edgar pulled his headlamp from his satchel.

"Sister, if he's underground, we'll find him."

They trudged through tunnel after tunnel, accompanied only by the sound of their feet on the wet limestone and the quiet gurgle of the canal. Edgar's lamp provided meagre light, and all they found were trails of mortar mix that they remembered spilling the previous night.

The tunnel split at last into three smaller ones. One led out a drainage pipe to the Running River, another led downtown, and the third led back home.

The twins took a few steps in each direction.

"I admit, Ellen – this Mason covered his tracks."

Ellen sighed and looked up at a grinning stone gargoyle perched in an alcove above. The winged monsters marked the major intersections of the tunnels, and over the years the twins had named them all. "Dear Yumley," she said, "if only *you* could tell us which direction that blasted Mason took."

"Yumley has seen more than he's letting on, Sister. Unless you've been marching around in boots, I've found something."

Edgar knelt on the homeward path and pointed his headlamp so Ellen could see. It was more mortar mix – this time imprinted with the heel of a boot.

"Well done, Brother," said Ellen. "The footprint betrays him."

"He was heading toward the Gadget Graveyard," said Edgar.

The twins found no further evidence as they followed the tunnel, and the closer they came to the graveyard exit, the more their uncertainty grew.

They were about to retrace their steps and search a different tunnel when they heard a metallic grinding sound up ahead.

Skreeeeeee – KLANG!

"A manhole cover! The Mason is escaping!" cried Edgar.

The twins raced toward the sound. Zigzag left, curve right – the tunnel twisted back and forth, but they soon reached the familiar passage that ended under the storm drain at the foot of Thaddeus Knightleigh's tomb.

"He could have escaped through any of the manholes between here and the mausoleum," said Ellen.

"There must be at least twenty," agreed Edgar. "He's long gone, no doubt."

They passed through the final archway of the tunnel, guarded by one last gargoyle. Wings spread and fangs bared, Horace sat above a stone on which was carved:

SMITHY & SONS
MASTER BUILDERS
NOD'S LIMBS
"Clean and sound
under town"
since 1780

Not a strictly accurate description these days, the twins often noted, but now their attention was drawn to the ground below the gargoyle. Atop the grime and muck lay a crumpled photograph.

11. The New Neighbours

The twins stared at the picture of gooey mayhem, and, in the middle of it all, themselves dancing.

"This is a most disturbing find," said Ellen. "It seems we've had a spy on our tail since the French Toast Festival."

"Let him try to steal from us again. He has no idea who he's wrangling with," said Edgar as they reached the ladder leading to the storm drain.

They emerged in the cemetery. As Edgar rolled the drain cover back into place, Ellen cried, "Look!" and yanked her brother's head around by the ear.

In the junkyard next door, several beefy men in yellow hardhats stood around a crane bearing the logo SMELTERBURG CONSTRUCTION CORPORATION. The men yelled and jumped out of the way as a steel beam crashed to the earth.

"Sorry!" shouted the crane driver.

"What are *they* doing in the Gadget Graveyard?" Ellen asked.

"Now we know who left us the bricks," said Edgar.

The twins clambered over the cemetery wall and marched up to the foreman, who observed the scene with his hands on his hips.

"What's going on here?" barked Ellen.

The man turned and glowered at them. The name "GUS" was scrawled on his hardhat and he chewed a fat wad of fruity-smelling gum.

"What's going on?" he repeated. "I'm kicking you out of here, that's what's going on. This is a work site. You need to play hide-and-seek somewhere else."

"This is our junkyard," said Ellen.

"Heh, heh. Not anymore, little missy," said the man. "This is where your Mayor Knightleigh is building his new hotel."

He pointed to a nearby poster that read "THE KNIGHTLORIAN HOTEL: LUXURIOUS VACATIONING IN NOD'S LIMBS – COMING SOON!" The sign depicted a towering lavender building that looked nearly identical to Edgar and Ellen's own house, except with shutters unbroken, windows clean, and shingles straight. Rather than a dried-up yard full of unpleasant and dying plants, there were charming gardens, a swimming pool, and a parking lot.

The twins' eyes widened. They had seen this drawing once before in the mayor's office. But they thought the events of the French Toast Festival had put an end to the mayor's scheme.

"They're… they're… actually going to build that monstrosity?" whispered Ellen.

"But we single-handedly ruined the tourism industry here," said Edgar. "I heard those VIPs say it: *'We never want to come here again.'* That Feemore woman declared Nod's Limbs a national hazard! How did this happen?"

"No more chitchat. It's time to work," said Gus, handing them a flyer from his vest pocket. "Just take this home to your parents."

"Don't let me catch you in here until the festival," Gus snarled. "This place isn't safe for you kids, got it?"

"Gee. Golly. Thanks, mister," said Edgar as he tore up the flyer.

Gus cracked his gum, waiting for the twins to scamper off. They didn't. He was about to speak when a ringing sounded from his vest. He pulled out a phone, spat out his gum, and motioned for the twins to stay quiet.

"No, sir, we haven't started yet," he said into the receiver. "Yes, the dump trucks were supposed to remove all this junk by now, but they're stuck in traffic on account of that bridge situation. . . Yes, sir. . . Sorry, sir." Gus turned off the phone and threw his hat on the ground. "It's not our fault we can't get to work. That Mason guy steals our bricks and then shuts down the only bridge that can support the weight of our trucks! Our guys can't cross. I knew we shouldn't have taken a job outside Smelterburg. Now beat it, you two!" As he walked off, he tripped over a runaway steel pipe.

"Simon!" he shouted. "Watch those pipes!"

"Sorry," called a worker.

"*We* stole those bricks," growled Ellen. She picked up Gus's wad of gum and pressed it firmly into his hat. "Let's give that gasbag a new hairdo."

"They can't haul off our treasure trove," said Edgar.

"Forget the junk," Ellen said suddenly. "What about Berenice?"

12. The Plight of Berenice

In a far corner of the junkyard, Edgar and Ellen stood over Berenice. Ellen had nurtured the carnivorous plant since her seedling days. For years Berenice flourished in a discarded mattress frame, and her thick vines now firmly encircled the metal bars, making her impossible to transplant. Her seeds were pointy and white and looked like teeth. Every evening, they fell to the ground, only to be replaced with new ones by morning. The twins had no explanation for this phenomenon, and Ellen's numerous attempts to plant the seeds failed to produce the slightest green shoot.

"Berenice, Berenice," sighed Ellen. "How can we move you out of here?"

She tugged at a few tight tendrils, but Berenice did not relax her grip. Instead, she swallowed a ladybird. Edgar smiled at the sizzle of digestion.

"What do you mean 'move her'?" he asked. "Why are you giving up Berenice's home so easily? This place is ours, and if Knightleigh wants it, he'll have to fight for it – medievally."

"Medievally?" asked Ellen. Then a thin grin spread over her face. "I see where you're going with this."

She looked at the photograph still in her hand.

"Don't worry, Mason," she said. "We'll take care of you as soon as Berenice is safe."

The twins spent the rest of the day in the forest sawing planks of wood, securing fasteners, and testing the durability of their catapult. Ellen repaired wobbly axles, while Edgar reinforced the crank handle.

Long after sunset, they sat back and reviewed their work.

"The aiming mechanism is still a little shaky," said Edgar, "and we can't crank the winch too far."

"You are such a perfectionist, Edgar," said Ellen. "The only important question is whether this catapult will fling cartloads of wing nuts, corkscrews, and beetle bugs on those who dare enter our junkyard."

"Nearly. One more day of toil, and we'll make it rain misery on those intruders. Get ready, Sister – we're going to wage a sleepless battle for Berenice."

13. Something's Amiss in the Junkyard

But when they approached the Gadget Graveyard the next morning, they noticed it was empty of people and trucks. The only activity came from Gus the foreman, who was pacing, waving his arms, and yelling into his phone again.

"Tell me something I don't know! I can see it from here. This is gonna set us back another day. Who ever heard of an isolated windstorm? I tell ya, this town is cursed!"

He snapped the phone shut and crammed several sticks of chewing gum in his mouth.

"Hi there, Gus," called Edgar. "Crew troubles?"

"Hey, you little brats," Gus said, hustling toward them. "I told you to stay out of here."

As he approached, the twins could see a scraggly, bald patch in the middle of his bushy hair that looked like a bare meadow in the Black Tree Forest Preserve. The construction foreman looked so flustered that Edgar snapped on his recorder to capture the ravings on tape.

"You two are as batty as this town," Gus spluttered. "Back home, children only wear pj's to bed. And they don't play in dangerous construction sites. Now scram, kiddies! Sheesh, I can't wait to finish the job and get back to Smelterburg. The way we're going, this hotel is doomed."

Ellen pulled Edgar away.

"Hey, I was getting great material there!"

"Forget your recorder," said Ellen. "What could possibly have set them back another day?"

"That," said Edgar, pointing to the sky. A column of dust and leaves – as well as odd, metallic flecks – swirled like a cyclone over the centre of town. The rest of the sky was clear and blue.

"More misery we didn't cause," said Ellen.

14. The Blustery Day

The twins rushed towards the whirling column of debris. Screaming winds led them to the river, where the colourful fall leaves had been prematurely swept from their branches and trees swayed naked in the gale. Dust and garbage whisked headlong down the road, joining the growing tornado twisting into the sky. Most curious of all was the trash itself – long strips of flimsy newsprint, glittery bits of foil, and fluorescent paper dots.

Confetti.

The confetti piled against parked cars, mailboxes, and doorsteps like snowdrifts in a blizzard. Cars and trucks sat immobile due to clogged wheel wells and buried windshields. As the twins observed the chaos, clusters of cheery paper scraps buried their feet and ankles. The air smelled funny, a slight but unmistakable odour Edgar quickly identified.

"Jet fuel," he said through teeth clenched partly out of frustration, partly to keep his mouth from filling with paper.

At the fringes of the storm, several citizens bravely tried to walk along the street, clutching their coats and squinting through the airborne grit. "How about this weather?" hollered one man to the twins before he fell on his rear and rolled away.

At last the twins saw what had made the foreman so angry. In the stalled traffic stood a line of Smelterburg Construction Corporation dump trucks, swamped to their headlights in confetti. The drivers peered out from windshields nearly blocked with sparkly trash.

Then, all at once, the wind died. Mrs Grundell's front-porch wind sock, laden with coloured paper, broke its string and dropped to the ground. Confetti drifted back to earth in the now-tranquil air.

"Party shrapnel," murmured Edgar.

15. Turbinal Velocity

While bystanders emerged from shops and homes to assess the damage, Edgar and Ellen sought the source of the mystery wind.

The twins stopped at the entrance to Betty LaFete's Hearty Party shop. They nodded to each other.

As they entered the store, Mrs LaFete looked up from behind the cash register and took off her headphones.

"Oh, you startled me," she said. "I hope you haven't been standing there very long. When I listen to my Wolfgang Amadeus, I get a little carried away. Now, how can I make your party hearty?"

The twins quickly scanned the walls and shelves.

"Aha!" cried Ellen. On the wall, a large, pointing hand contained the words "BETTY'S CONFETTI:

HANDMADE WITH LOVE. WAREHOUSE AND BULK SALES THIS WAY!"

They followed the sign to the party shop's second-floor loft. Mrs LaFete hurried after them, calling, "Children! What's going on?" Then she stopped and gasped. The loft was empty, and a large window was open.

"My confetti!" she wailed. "Where's my confetti?"

She rushed about, groping the air as if her supply had merely turned invisible and needed only a good squeeze to reappear. Edgar and Ellen, however, understood at once. Against the back wall, directed toward the open window, sat a large, rusty turbine engine, the very one the twins salvaged from the Gadget Graveyard months earlier.

"That's *our* turbine," said Ellen.

"That's *our idea*," said Edgar. "This whole thing is disturbingly similar to my plan for Operation: Whiplash. Remember?"

"This stinks like wet Pet hair, Edgar."

Suddenly, the twins heard a cry and a *thud*. They turned and saw Mrs LaFete sprawled on the floor.

"Fainted?" said Edgar. "It's only confetti – it's not like she can't make more."

"It wasn't the crime that shocked her," said Ellen as she pried something from Mrs LaFete's hands. "It was the criminal."

She held up a red brick. Chiselled in precise letters were the words "THE MASON."

16. Retracing Steps

"I searched every crevice in this house," said Edgar as he descended the ladder from the attic-above-the-attic. "Every drawing, every scrap of paper, every wadded-up napkin with a brilliant idea sketched on it – all missing. Stolen."

"Stealing *our* plans from *our* house!" said Ellen. "Stealing is wrong. Immoral! Only *we* should get away with it."

"We need to find that Mason and fix him for good." Edgar reached deep into his satchel and pulled out the handheld tape recorder. "This will help us crack the case. All great detectives keep track of the details as they pursue jewel thieves and smugglers."

"A regular Sherlock, aren't you?" muttered Ellen.

"You make a great Watson," said Edgar, "always a step behind." He pressed the record button. "Tuesday, 8am. The rain was coming down hard when I saw the confetti. Right away I knew this was no ordinary assailant I was up against. Then again, I was no ordinary man—"

"It wasn't even raining!" cried Ellen. She turned and stomped away. "Bah! Have fun with your toy, Edgar. I have real work to do."

"Where are you going?"

"Back to the place where we found the photograph. Maybe we missed something."

"Hmm," said Edgar. "Not a bad idea... for an amateur."

The twins started for the sewers and began to sing:

> What a nervy, scurvy louse,
> What gall to break into our house!
> We'll find this rogue and then we'll roust
> Him from his secret swindling.
> But this Mason's made a blunder.
> Let him try to thieve our thunder,
> Turn our plans into his plunder!
> This rascal's days are dwindling.

17. To the Sewers and Beyond

Underground, however, further clues proved hard to find. After an hour of examining a fifty-foot section of walkway, the twins had turned up nothing. At last, Ellen yawned and wandered away.

"Don't give up yet, Ellen," said Edgar, who continued crawling on all fours. "We may still find some forensic evidence."

"Do you even know what *forensic* means?"

Edgar ignored her and continued to search the limestone floor. Ellen strolled along the tunnel, running her hand over the blackened wall. Slimy moss covered its cracks and gaps and squished pleasantly under her hands. She pinched the green sponge, peeling strips off the wall as she walked and dropping them on the ground.

Squish, splat. Squish, splat. Squish, splat. SQUISH.

"What have we here?" said Ellen. The moss had changed from thin to bushy. She inspected the wall more closely and noticed a thick green carpet growing from floor to ceiling – but only for a short distance. The rest of the wall was mostly bare.

She detected a faint but strange odour that could not be the moss and she peered closer. In one spot, someone had scraped away the plant life where a sliver of rock jutted out.

"Hello," she muttered, pushing the sliver into the wall. A large panel swung aside, revealing a dark passageway beyond.

"Hey, Mr Detective," said Ellen. "Look at this."

18. Hollowed Ground

"The old Release-Mechanism-Disguised-as-Innocent-Rock trick," said Edgar. "An ancient ruse, but effective."

The tunnel behind the door was lower and narrower than other sewer passages, with a crumbling ceiling and an uneven floor of loose dirt and rocks. The walls bore the rough marks of a pickaxe, suggesting someone had widened them by hand.

"I will say one thing for the Mason," said Edgar. "He has an excellent hideout."

"He's also got our plans," said Ellen. "So get moving."

As Edgar and Ellen crept through the cramped tunnel, small streams of dirt occasionally poured from the ceiling into their hair and eyes.

"We must be near our house!" murmured Ellen. "The Mason's lair has been close to us all along."

The air was stale and still, but with each step, they inhaled stronger and stronger whiffs of the unusual odour Ellen detected in the moss. It smelled earthy, but with a sweet overtone, like the rotting rind of a cantaloupe. They couldn't place the scent or decide if it was pleasant or foul.

After about twenty yards, the tunnel opened into a wide, high chamber. The light from Edgar's headlamp disappeared in the gloomy expanse. Ellen clapped her hands once – a single low *boom* sounded in the darkness.

After a few long seconds, the echoes came shuddering back.

"Sinister. I like it," she said.

Edgar cautiously led the way into the cavern. The deeper they ventured, the stronger the strange scent became. Suddenly the floor disappeared, and Edgar stepped into nothingness.

"The end!" he cried, teetering on the brink.

"Watch it," hissed Ellen, pulling her brother back to safety. "No falling down holes unless I push you."

The twins peered over the edge. The hole was tremendously wide and when Edgar took a marble

from his satchel and dropped it in, they never heard it hit the bottom.

Edgar gulped and gestured to his right. "Let's be a little more careful, shall we?"

The twins moved deeper into the cave. After a few paces, the reflection of something shiny winked back at them in the distance. As they neared, shapes emerged in the headlamp's beam: tables and shelves filled with glasses and bottles; instruments constructed of copper pipes and rusty metal; a web of wires and tubes connecting many of the unusual devices together.

"Sister," Edgar said, "This is a *laboratory*."

19. A Lab in the Dark

"The Mason must be some kind of mad scientist. I don't even recognize most of this equipment." Edgar pointed to a closed wooden box with a crank on its side like a hand organ. "What does this thing do?"

"Let's find out." Ellen began to turn the crank. The box let out tortured squeaks, like the sound of metal spikes dragging across glass. Blue sparks crackled between the copper wires coming from the box.

"Keep cranking!" called Edgar. He followed the wires from the box to a rack of murky jars. Gray fluid in the jars pulsed with each turn of the handle — and then he spied the switch beside the rack.

"Stand by for ignition," he said, "or perhaps just something fiery and painful." He threw the switch.

With a buzz and a crackle, egg-shaped bulbs on the walls filled the room with light. Ellen's cranking arm fell limp. The lab covered half the giant cavern and was filled with far more equipment than they had seen in the feeble glow of the headlamp: corked jars, test tubes, books, yellowed papers, and unidentifiable instruments covered table after table; extinguished burners sat beneath bulbous flasks with long necks; crumbling rubber tubes ran through a series of beakers.

A white film coated every container and contraption. In places it was thin and flaky, but where it was thick, it was moist, like half-dried glue. This seemed to be the source of the mysterious odour.

"Is our Mason a paste manufacturer?" asked Ellen, trying to wipe a glob from her finger.

"Perhaps he's going to use this gunk to seal us inside our house," said Edgar as he wandered through the room, testing levers and twisting knobs. He picked up a pair of cast-iron tongs connected to thick electric cables. "Ah, here's a nasty device. Maybe he plans to torture us."

"Hmm. From the looks of it, he doesn't spend much time down here," said Ellen. "Everything is covered with dust."

"Charming, isn't it?" said Edgar. "Better take some of these things for analysis." He opened his satchel and tossed in anything that fitted: a chisel, the iron tongs, beakers, and Erlenmeyer flasks.

"Look – he recently disturbed some of the dust on these tables," Ellen said. "And if you hadn't just stepped all over the floor, I might have been able to

follow his footprints. You made a mixed-up jumble of it all."

Edgar took out his tape recorder. "10am. The mystery deepens," he said. Ellen sighed heavily. "We have uncovered the Mason's lair, where he fiendishly schemes to steal the ideas of those more capable than himself. Alas, he is a terrible housekeeper, and I fear the stench and dust are hampering Ellen's brain; she complains of feeling mixed up and jumbled. Will she be a liability to our hunt?"

A beaker sailed within inches of his head, crashing against the cavern wall. "Quit *playing* detective, Edgar, and start acting like one."

Edgar paused to scan a bookshelf and read the titles aloud. *"The Opus Paradoxium, On Conquering Matter, Alchemy for Village Idiots* – this is all humbug and crackpot science. What kind of scientist *is* this guy?"

His eyes fell upon a book that lay open on the desk. Elegant script filled the yellow pages. "The Mason's own journal!" he called, snatching it up.

"All his little secrets will be in there, Brother," said Ellen. "We've got him now!"

"Dear Diary," Edgar said in a mocking voice. "Today I took something that didn't belong to me, and now angry twins are about to give me the thrashing I so richly deserve."

The twins sat down to read, singing:

> *Far beneath the surface lie*
> *Forgotten mysteries left to die.*
> *"Secrets! Secrets!" caverns cry,*
> *Sunk deep for us to find.*
> *So now we launch an inquiry*
> *Into this dusty diary—*
> *Who's the Mason? Here's our key*
> *To reading through his mind.*

20. Notes from Underground

Edgar flipped the pages, and the book fell open to a passage somewhere in the middle. The pages crackled, as if they had not been disturbed for some time.

The thickness of the ink faded in and out, like someone had written the words with a feather quill. The twins leaned in and read:

2 July

Further experimentation goes nowhere. I have endured weeks without a breakthrough. The substance simply does not react the way I expect! To further delay my progress, the equipment has required frequent repairs. The Voltaic Electro–Generator holds less and less of a charge; thus I must crank more often to power the bulbs. Even so, I quite prefer bulb light to candles, which (as clearly demonstrated by the events of 12 April) are much more dangerous when working with the balm. Oh, Fates! Do not abandon me in this bleak hour. Muses, do not deny me inspiration.

Despair!

"Boring," said Ellen. "Skip to the part where he steals our stuff."

But when Edgar paged forward, the book opened
to a hand-drawn map.

All Hallows' Eve

*I have discovered a most troublesome weak-
ness in the security of my underground
laboratory.*

*Narrow tunnels weave through the ground
under the forest and cemetery, creating a
vast honeycomb. I have just discovered that
one of these tunnels connects my laboratory*

to a hole in the Black Tree Forest. Any man, as he wanders these woods in deep thought, may tumble down and find me as I work. I must seal this breach to protect my secret laboratory. Or perhaps I shall build a structure above it to conceal the hole from K— and other sinister parties who seek to learn more about my work.

"Sneaky, sneaky," said Ellen. "He doesn't have to use the sewers to get here – he has direct access from some building above."

"Let's go knock on his door," said Edgar.

21. On the Warpath

With the map in hand, finding this exit proved simple. The bulbs cast a flickering glow across the grand cavern as the twins filed over to a far wall. When they came to another, narrower cave, however, the lights went out with a *zzzzzzzz*.

"Hmm. Short fuse. Just like yours," said Edgar. He put on his headlamp.

Edgar and Ellen began a steep ascent to the surface. Just as the diary warned, this new cave resembled a honeycomb. Tunnels forked and doubled back on themselves. Lesser explorers might have got lost in the maze, wandering until they died beneath the earth.

The twins felt right at home. They immediately spied a faint rut in the ground, made by years of someone travelling through the caves.

They followed this path through the labyrinth until they reached a dead end. Edgar searched the wall for some clue, until Ellen nudged him and pointed to the ceiling. Above them, they saw a wooden trapdoor.

"Vengeance is at hand," she whispered.

She placed a foot in a nook between the rocks and pulled herself up to the door. It was quite heavy, but it clattered open at last, and dust rained on their faces.

The twins heaved themselves through the opening. The room they entered was quite small, with a cot, a door, and a single grime-covered window. Ellen took a few steps forward, but Edgar stared intently around the room. Something about the crack in the window seemed strangely familiar to him.

"A voice in my head cries 'Abandon ship,'" Edgar said, "but I'm not sure why."

Then he saw the accordion.

22. The Inner Sanctum

The twins had never seen beyond the window of Heimertz's shed; going inside was never even a consideration. They clutched each other.

"*Heimertz* is the Mason!" said Ellen, whose excited whisper rose nearly to a shout. "This is very bad."

"Worse than bad," said Edgar. "He's been watching us all these years, learning our methods. He knows everything about us!"

Edgar was sure he and his sister could square off against most anyone. But Heimertz? He shivered.

"Well," said Ellen, "we're not backing down now. Heimertz has made himself our sworn enemy." Her voice wavered a bit.

"Let's search for our things before he comes back."

Ellen nodded. "You keep watch by the window while I poke around."

"What? *You* keep watch. Those are *my* plans he stole."

"Keep your voice down! You're closer to the window. Just keep a lookout, and we'll be out of here in minutes."

Edgar began to argue, but an unearthly squawk from outside stopped him. He peered out the window, his heart hammering.

"Just a crow," he whispered. "Okay, I'll keep watch. But be quick about it."

With trembling hands, Ellen opened the drawers of a decrepit nightstand, but the contents only confused her further: a drained snow globe with an elephant inside; a plunger with no handle; seven blunt toothpicks; three half-empty jars of apricot preserve.

"There," said Edgar, pointing to an open steamer trunk. "I see some rolled-up papers."

"Eyes out the window!" snapped Ellen.

She poked around the trunk, pulling out a large roll of paper. What she unfurled was not Edgar's drawings, however. It was a collection of circus posters.

"Curious," she said, raising an eyebrow.

"Where are those plans?" said Edgar. "This place isn't big enough to hide all the stuff he stole from us."

"If I have to tell you again about that window—"
A faint clomping noise choked off her voice. Heavy footsteps drew closer to the shed, and the twins knew

– after years of hiding at the very sound – that these footsteps signalled the approach of the caretaker.

The doorknob slowly turned, and the twins dived for the opening in the floor. Shoving elbows into each other's ribs, they tumbled headlong into the tunnel below. The trapdoor slammed shut behind them – but only Ellen landed on the ground. She looked up to see Edgar dangling upside down above her, the left toe of his footie pyjamas caught in the heavy door.

23. Smelt

Heimertz stood in his doorway, filling the frame with his bulk. He wore the same grease-stained overalls and wide smile as always. In his right hand, he held an axe with a severely chipped blade.

Meanwhile, Ellen stood on the ledge beneath the trapdoor, tugging Edgar's foot as quietly as possible. Through a crack in the boards, she saw the caretaker step closer. Edgar swung helplessly, sweat beading on his forehead.

The big, blank grin didn't flicker. But then Heimertz jerked his head and began sniffing in all directions. He sucked in a breath and then drew another, longer and slower than the first. He stepped closer to the trapdoor, crouching and snuffling like a bloodhound.

He knelt directly over Ellen's face – their noses could not have been more than a foot apart, and Ellen's eyes began to water as Heimertz's face filled the gaps between the narrow floorboards. She cowered in the shadows as his eyes darted left and right, and then, with a final snort, he stood abruptly. Heimertz's smile tightened and his eyes bulged.

The change in his expression was nearly imperceptible. For Heimertz, however, it was like a whole new face.

Ellen bit her tongue and threw her full weight onto Edgar's leg. His footie came free with a loud *riiiiiip,* and both twins plummeted to the ground and fled.

24. Prankster's Block

Back in their seventh-floor den, Edgar paced while Ellen plucked beetles from her potted pigweed.

"We can hang him upside down from the attic window," said Ellen, dropping another beetle into a jam jar.

"How will we get him through the window? No, we should barricade him in his shed and not let him out until he returns our plans."

"Except that he has a trapdoor that leads to the sewers *beneath his bed!*"

"Wait — I've got it!" said Edgar. "With a bucket of molasses and a ten-foot pole—"

"No," said Ellen.

Various sketches on the wall depicted all types of attacks against their new enemy. One plan showed Heimertz coated in caramel and rolled in corn as chickens pecked angrily at him. After two hours of discussion, this was their most workable idea. Edgar cracked his knuckles and scowled.

Every time they dared peek out the window, they saw Heimertz below, sitting on a tree stump looking back at them. In the hours since they escaped through the trapdoor, Heimertz had not moved from this stump or averted his eyes. No matter where the twins retreated, it seemed Heimertz already stared directly at the window from which they peered.

"Maybe it's better to just get it over with," suggested Edgar. "Some kind of surprise attack?"

"True, the longer we wait, the harder this will be," said Ellen. "It's like pulling duct tape off your eyebrows. Best to charge ahead and do it without thinking too much."

"Exactly," said Edgar, then frowned as he rubbed a bald spot on his own eyebrow. "So, go to it, Sister. Surprise him."

"I'm really not a very surprising person, Brother. You are *much* better at surprises than I."

"Not true – I am constantly surprised by your ignorance and clumsiness."

Ellen jumped up to pounce on Edgar, then caught a glimpse out the window.

"He's gone!" she gasped.

"Surprise," Edgar muttered.

25. Erratic Behaviours

A slight rustle came from the hallway. Edgar reached into a trunk and seized the ankle of an artificial leg. He leaped through the doorway, waving the limb like a sword.

"Have at thee!"

To his amazement, Edgar saw only a small ball of hair on the stairwell.

"Hmph. Hello, Pet," said Edgar. "Since when do *you* come looking for *us?*" Indeed, it was quite unusual for Pet to allow itself to be caught in the open. Over the years, Pet had been the victim of much torment. Its sluggishness and passive nature made it a marvellous paintbrush, shuttlecock, toilet clogger, and all-around boredom reliever. It seemed not to relish this kind of abuse, so it was strange that Pet should suddenly appear.

"Scram, Pet," said Ellen. "We're busy."

Edgar threw the artificial limb aside and returned to his seat to think. A moment later, he felt something brush up against him.

"Pet?" Edgar asked. Sure enough, Pet had sidled up to Edgar and was now sitting on his foot. "Confound it, why would you pick today to go loopy? Shove off!"

He launched Pet out of the room with a flex of his knee.

"It's out of its hairy little head," said Edgar, slamming the door.

"*We're* the ones about to attack Heimertz," said Ellen. "We're probably out of *our* heads too. But we have no choice." She pushed up the sleeves of her pyjamas and marched off with the stride of a matador entering the arena to face an enormous bull. Edgar swallowed hard, then followed her down the stairs, singing:

> *Dauntless, daring, down we go,*
> *Off to meet our fearsome foe,*
> *A tricky one he's proven, so*

To catch him we must hasten—
We must stop his knavery
And though it's quite unsavoury,
Now's the time for bravery
Since Heimertz is the Mason!

When they threw open the front door of their home – still without the slightest idea of what they were going to do – the grounds were quiet. Twilight had settled, deepening the shadows in the scrubby yard.

"Where are you, Heimertz?" called Ellen from the front door. "Come out and face us, *Mason!*"

Edgar cracked his knuckles. His eyes strained to pick out any movement, but all was still.

More cracking.

"Quit it, Edgar," said Ellen. "I'm trying to listen."

"That wasn't me," said Edgar. The twins spun around.

Heimertz stood inside the house, not ten feet behind them. He held a bowl full of peanuts and shoved a handful into his mouth, shells and all. His blank eyes met theirs as he crunched loudly, baring his teeth with each smiley bite.

26. Fish in a Barrel

Edgar stumbled backwards off the porch. He grabbed Ellen's pigtail to save himself, but succeeded only in toppling the both of them. Edgar fell head-first into an empty rainwater barrel, with Ellen landing on top of him.

"Get off me!" called Edgar from the bottom of the barrel. "He's coming after us!"

"Now who's the clumsy one?" yelled Ellen. "You're going to get us killed!"

She struggled to get out, but the commotion threw the barrel off balance, and it tipped and rolled onto the lawn.

For Edgar, up became down and down up. His sister blocked his escape in one direction. Rotting wooden boards, which on the whole seemed easier to reckon with, blocked the other. He pressed his feet against the side of the barrel, lowered his shoulder, and plowed forward.

Rotting chunks of timber shot in all directions, and the metal hoops holding the planks together clattered to the ground. Edgar found himself looking up at the twilight stars with a mouth full of slivers.

"The hoops!" he sputtered.

"Way ahead of you," said Ellen as she sprung from the wreckage with one of the metal rings in her hand.

The twins raced up the front steps and through the door. Heimertz stood right where they had left him, impassively munching his peanuts.

"How dare you steal our stuff!" cried Ellen. She leapt at Heimertz's head.

"Suffer, fiend!" yelled Edgar, a pace behind.

With that, two metal rings slipped over Heimertz's head and down his thick arms, where they cinched tightly and bound his elbows to his sides. Through it all, Heimertz chewed and smiled with nary a twitch. Despite the grip of the rings, he continued tossing peanuts into his mouth.

Panting and shaking, Edgar turned to Ellen.

"I… guess we have him."

"Yes, I guess we do."

"Now what?"

"Beats me."

27. Good Twin, Bad Twin

The twins stood back from the caretaker as if he were a ticking bomb.

"Ask him," whispered Ellen.

"Me? Why me?" asked Edgar.

"Because I've already saved your life once today. It's your turn."

Edgar scowled but nonetheless turned to the caretaker.

"We know you're the Mason," he said, unable to stop the trembling in his voice. "We know you stole our designs. Where are they? Confess!"

Heimertz only smiled.

"We can make life very difficult for you if you don't cooperate," said Ellen.

Edgar grabbed a high-powered flashlight from the hall closet and hopped on a chair that put him level with Heimertz. He shone the light into the caretaker's eyes.

"Where are our plans? Why are you working against us? *Don't make me get the chickens!*" he shrieked, his own face not six inches from his adversary's. Heimertz didn't blink and his toothy grin never wavered. But Edgar's hand did, and the flashlight beam slipped to Heimertz's shiny teeth, reflecting back into Edgar's eyes.

"Ack!" screeched Edgar. "I'm blind! I'm blind!" He fell off the chair and rolled across the floor.

Heimertz remained motionless.

"Edgar, you are *embarrassing* us," hissed Ellen, pulling her brother to his feet. She led him out the front door. "Let's try a different tack."

She took a deep breath and returned to the unmoving Heimertz.

"I'm – I'm sorry about my brother. He has a tendency to act rashly in tense situations." Ellen dragged the chair near – but not too near – Heimertz and sat down. She leaned an elbow on a side table, striking an unconcerned pose.

"You know, I'd really like to take those barrel hoops off you, but Edgar, he's determined to keep you here, maybe put you through something worse. I know he was eyeing those tongs you keep in your lab."

This was, by far, the most Ellen had ever spoken to Heimertz. Her throat felt dry but she persisted.

"Maybe if you just told me a few minor details – like, why are you imitating us? You can tell me that, right? That's not much – I can feed that to my brother, and maybe he'll agree to take the hoops off so we can move this conversation someplace more comfortable."

Heimertz shifted his weight from his left foot to his right. The sudden movement made Ellen flinch. She desperately wanted a glass of water. She chewed her lip and continued.

"This can all go away…"

Suddenly, Edgar burst in and slammed his fists on the table.

Ellen jumped.

Heimertz didn't.

"You will tell us what we want to know, or you'll stand there all night, you good for nothing… *desperado!*"

His voice cracked on the word "desperado."

Edgar's threat, however, turned out to be true. Hours crept by, and no amount of pleading, cajoling, or annoying could make Heimertz talk or even dim his everlasting grin. The twins discovered that Heimertz was not allergic to pigweed pollen or averse to chilli peppers, didn't mind being spritzed with a spray bottle, and made no response to Ellen shrieking in his ear or Edgar poking him with an umbrella.

He was a rock.

28. The Last Straw

"Maybe he has no vocal cords," suggested Edgar after all their tactics had failed.

"That, Brother, is a rare excellent point from you," said Ellen. She retrieved paper and pen, laid them in front of Heimertz on the table, and quickly backed away.

"Write down where our plans are."

Heimertz reached for the paper. Edgar and Ellen watched intently. Despite his pinned arms, he deftly folded the sheet into an origami alligator and carefully placed it on the table.

Edgar was soon halfheartedly flicking Heimertz's earlobes.

"Look what we've been reduced to," moaned Ellen.

"We've been going about this all wrong," said Edgar. "It's all a matter of leverage—"

"I told you, Edgar," interrupted Ellen. "The *leverager* has to threaten something precious to the *leveragee*. We have nothing of the sort!"

Edgar thought for a moment, then dashed into the yard.

He was back in an instant carrying a hammer and a bulky object hidden by a pillowcase.

"All right, the time for pleasantries is over. If you don't tell us what we want to know," he pulled the pillowcase off, revealing Heimertz's accordion, "the polka machine gets it!" He dropped the instrument on the table and raised the hammer above his head.

Heimertz's smile didn't fade, but with a flex of his biceps, he shattered the barrel hoops that bound him. Edgar dropped the hammer on the floor as the caretaker snatched up his beloved accordion and lumbered out of the front door.

Lively polka strains wafted from Heimertz's shed as the first rays of light peeked over the house.

29. The Mason Strikes Again

"That went better than expected," said Ellen.

"What are you talking about?" said Edgar. "We still don't have our plans, and Heimertz is free to keep up his Mason charade. We don't even know *why* he's doing it."

"That's better than getting pounded into rat food, isn't it?"

As the twins retreated up the stairs, Edgar tripped over something on the second-floor landing.

"Criminy, Pet, what has gotten into you? BEAT IT!" he yelled. But Pet just nuzzled Edgar's foot.

"That's it. I hereby withdraw your freedom privileges!" Edgar grabbed Pet and stormed up to the seventh-floor den, where an empty birdcage hung in a corner.

"You're getting a time-out," Edgar said, throwing the creature into the cage and slamming the door. He could still hear the discordant refrain of the accordion through an open window.

"Tuneless hack!" he called, and switched on the television to drown out the sound. The Nod's Limbs Public Access Channel came onto the screen.

At this early hour, Tug Wollmers, host of *The Morning Farm Report with Tug Wollmers,* was brightly informing his listeners about the rising price of pigs' feet, when he was cut off in midsentence by an announcement:

"We interrupt this broadcast for a special report from Nod's Limbs Public Access Action Eyewitness News!"

Ellen joined Edgar in front of the television.

"Now what?" she asked.

"This is Natalie Nickerson for Action Eyewitness News with your 'News for Now'. I'm here at the construction site of the Knightlorian Hotel, where another act of depravity by the Mason has blighted our fair town."

Natalie Nickerson, a perky young correspondent with perfectly sculpted hair, stood before the mounds of junk that Edgar and Ellen recognized so well. At the bottom of the screen, a colourful logo read "THE MARK OF THE MASON: A TOWN UNDER SIEGE."

"Details are sketchy at the moment," she continued, "but we do know that about thirty active beehives were stolen from the Nod's Limbs Zoo late last night. Those beehives seem to have been thrown—" She raised a hand to her ear. "No, I'm being told now that

they were catapulted – is that right? Catapulted? –
catapulted about an hour ago into the junkyard you
see behind me."

In the background, the twins made out men in
yellow hardhats rushing about, swatting the air and
scurrying on all fours. They tripped and stumbled
over the shattered hives.

"I don't know if you folks at home can see this on
your screens, but the air behind me is filled with angry
bees. Those little guys are sure upset."

The twins gawked at the television. They saw
Berenice in the background, happily snapping at the
swarms.

"I'm told we have some footage coming from the
Black Tree Forest Preserve on the other side of Ricketts
Road." The station cut away from Natalie Nickerson
to images of the catapult – but it was not entirely the
twins' handiwork on display.

"He fixed our catapult," said Ellen. "How rude."

Natalie Nickerson continued: "This seems to be
the handmade device that was used to launch the
beehives. And... is that what I think it is?" The camera zoomed in on the ground behind the catapult.
"Nod preserve us! Yet another brick with the words
THE MASON carved into it. Shocking."

Edgar's clenched fists shook and Ellen ground her teeth.

"Let's talk to an eyewitness. Sir?" The reporter approached Gus the foreman who, the twins noticed, wore his hardhat clamped down on his head. "Hi, Natalie Nickerson with Action Eyewitness News. What did you see here this morning?"

Gus chomped his gum, swatting at a circling bee. "A whole lot of angry bees!"

"And did you see anyone lurking about suspiciously? Anyone who might have been the Menacing Mason?"

The foreman grunted. "The only thing I saw was a shower of beehives falling from the sky." The bee landed on Gus's cheek and crawled toward his mouth. "Look, I don't know what's going on but this whole town is out of whack. Back in Smelterburg, we call this place Nod's Loons – and now I know why!"

Suddenly, the bee dashed for Gus's gum, flying right into the foreman's mouth. Gus yelped as the bee dug its stinger into his tongue.

Natalie Nickerson backed away from the crazed foreman, who was now hopping around in pain and clutching his tongue.

"So… there you have it – the Monstrous Mason continues his reign of terror. More news flashes as they become available. Now, back to your morning farm report!"

Ellen punched the sofa. "Edgar! That couldn't have been the work of Heimertz," she said. "He was here all night. He's still playing that accordion now. He couldn't have stolen the beehives or vaulted them into the Gadget Graveyard."

Edgar replied softly, "I cannot *believe* we just attacked Heimertz for no reason. That was very, very dumb."

"Yes, but the genuine offender is a normal human again," said Ellen. "And that means we can outsmart him."

"The chase is back on, Sister!"

"The Mason is doomed!"

30. Unusual Suspects

"If Heimertz isn't our culprit, we need to do more sleuthing," said Edgar.

"As long as Berenice has a blissful day to gorge herself on bees, we have time to put an end to this impostor," said Ellen. "But where do we begin?"

"First, we need to make a list of suspects. Then we'll figure out the motive," said Edgar.

When they were finished, they had an impressive list:

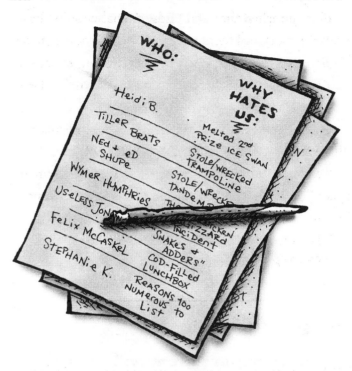

"Now for the detective work," said Edgar, reading over Ellen's shoulder. "Cross off the people who couldn't possibly have stolen our stuff. The last name left on the list is our villain."

"Fine," said Ellen. "Let's start with anyone who isn't smart enough to pull off these elaborate pranks."

Edgar and Ellen stared thoughtfully at the list.

"That covers everybody," said Edgar. His sister wadded up the papers and threw them away.

31. Read Any Good Books Lately?

"Maybe it's time for another look at the diary," said Ellen.

Edgar retrieved the journal from his satchel in the front hall closet.

"Let's start with his last entry this time," he said.

Mid–September (or is it October? – I no longer know)

I am driven to seek a better understanding of the balm. My obsession has led me to live a life apart from the town, and at last I feel I am near an incredible discovery. To take the next step, I must delve into the deep again and gather more of the substance – much more than I have gathered in a long,

long time. Over the years, I have harvested untold quantities from the spring, yet it never seems to empty. Blessed be! Where would I be without it? Interesting— Pilosoculus watches me intently, now more than ever. Is it worried about me? Sweet little thing. I shall let it sleep tomorrow when I go on my excursion. This trip may be dangerous, and I can't bear risking a hair on its hirsute little head.

"What is he talking about?" said Ellen. "This has nothing to do with our stolen plans."

"Ellen," said her brother, "have you noticed how all the Mason's attacks have stopped those construction lunkheads in their tracks?"

"So they have," she said, rubbing her pinkie. "He must be trying to save the Gadget Graveyard! He has our plans – *now* he wants our treasure."

"No, no, no. His lab!" said Edgar. "He's trying to protect it – and whatever this balm stuff is. It's clearly the most important thing to him. And when they start digging the hotel's foundation, they might discover his headquarters."

A loud crash from the basement made them jump.

"Heimertz?" whispered Edgar.

The twins flipped on the basement lights and peered in. Edgar followed Ellen down the stairs.

A rickety folding chair lay sprawled on its side.

"Odd," said Ellen.

The door to the subbasement was open, and a familiar hairball sat on the top step.

"It's Pet! How did it get out of the birdcage?"

"I don't know," said Ellen, "but it pushed this chair over. What are you doing, Pet?" She picked up the creature and held it over the stair railing.

"You daring devil, bungee jumping without a rope," she said, letting Pet fall. It hit the floor with a *thumph*.

"Seeing Pet tumble never loses its charm," said Edgar.

"Indeed. Let's try that again."

Ellen felt her footie stick slightly to each step as she descended.

Pet had landed in a pile of white, smelly gunk in front of the large wine casks where the twins first found it years ago. As she stooped to pick it up, she saw a shoe print on the dusty floor next to the gummy mound.

"Brother, there's something here you might want to see," she called.

Edgar ran down. "What is it?"

"Right here, next to Pet."

Edgar knelt, placing a hand on a cask to steady himself.

But steady he was not. The face of the wooden cask swung outward on a hinge, and Edgar fell on his face.

"Another door!" Ellen exclaimed.

Pet, who before this day never showed interest in anything besides television and hiding from the twins, scuttled toward the open cask. It moved faster than Edgar and Ellen had ever seen it go. Ellen only just managed to grab its scruff before it darted through the door.

"Did you see that?" she cried.

"It was speedier than Miss Croquet the day we tossed that bag of newts into the teachers' lounge," said Edgar as he opened his satchel. "Must be trying to escape. Shove it in here."

With Pet crammed inside the bag, the twins stepped into the cask and slammed the door shut behind them.

One would expect the inside of an oaken cask to be, well… casklike. Instead, the twins found themselves on stairs carved out of rock. A faint light flickered below, and a now-familiar odour filled the air. They climbed down the steps and emerged in a cavernous room lit by antique glass bulbs.

Edgar gasped. "The Mason's lab!"

"Not just near our house – connected to it!" said Ellen, shaking her head. "The *nerve*."

Suddenly, the satchel began to twitch as Pet frantically knocked against the sides. Edgar gave the bag a vigorous shake.

"Be still, nuisance," he said, and turned back to his sister. "This is how the Mason stole our plans and our turbine. It was all so easy – he invaded us from below!"

"Edgar, look – the lights are on. When I cranked that contraption before, the power lasted only a few minutes. That means—"

"He was just here," Edgar finished.

32. Man's Best Friend Is a Bee

Above ground, Mayor Knightleigh shuffled nervously as a large flatbed truck rolled into the junkyard. Three men got out of the cab. The names "WENDELL," "WALLY," and "STILLMAN" were embroidered on the breast pockets of their spotless white overalls.

"Finally. Exterminators. Where have you been?" asked the mayor. "We have a pest *emergency* and I want these bees out of my building site, pronto!"

"Exterminators?" asked Stillman in a soft voice. "Oh no, sir. No, no, no – we're the beekeepers." He glanced around the junkyard, where swarms of angry insects whizzed in all directions. "We're from the zoo. Dr Von Barlow sent us. We've come to bring our little fellows back."

"Listen to me," Mayor Knightleigh said. "I've got to get construction crews in here today, and I have a photo shoot for the newspaper this afternoon – these bees need to be evicted right away. Do you have some sort of vacuum to suck them out? Toxic spray? A bee swatter?"

The beekeepers gasped.

"That won't be necessary, sir," said Stillman calmly. "We just need to talk to them a little. Things will be right as rain in a jiffy."

"Talk... to them?" asked the mayor. "No, no talking. Killing! Squashing!" A bee landed on the mayor's sleeve. He shrieked and raised his hand to swat it away.

"Careful, sir!" said Wendell. "That's Rupert."

"There, there, Rupert. He wasn't going to hit you," said Wally, collecting the bee on his finger and smoothing its wings.

"In an hour, our friends will be home where they belong, and you can get back to building your hotel," said Stillman.

"Truly?" The mayor looked doubtful.

"We know our bees, sir."

33. Pray for the Prey

The twins left the Mason's lab and entered the sewer. Pet had ceased its thrashing, so Edgar opened his satchel a crack and slipped out his headlamp. The yellow light blinked awake, but immediately began to fade.

"Oh, no! Not *now!*" said Edgar. The bulb winked out, stranding the twins in total darkness.

"Hush," hissed Ellen. "I heard something."

Scurrying feet echoed through the walkway to their left.

"Follow me!" Ellen whispered.

The soft *flippity-flap* of their footie pyjamas echoed across the vaulted ceilings and down the corridors. But those were not the only sounds. Hundreds of *scritchy scratches* sounded around them, and Ellen felt something scurry over her foot.

"Oh, rats," she said.

"What's wrong?" asked Edgar.

"Rats. Rodents. Sewer pigeons. Not the Mason." A wave of the creatures swelled past her, and Ellen hopped aside to avoid them. She landed on the edge of the canal and teetered, wildly waving her arms to regain her balance. Just as her body began to pitch into the foul water, she felt a hand grab her left pigtail and pull her back. She fell onto the stone floor, gasping for breath.

"Thanks, Edgar, you owed me one," she said as her rescuer dashed off at full speed. "Where are you going?"

"What do you mean?" asked Edgar. "I'm over here – shaking a rat out of my footie."

"Edgar!" she cried. "He was right beside me! *The Mason pulled my hair!*"

She glimpsed a weak shaft of light from a far-off manhole cover; the light wavered as a shape ran by.

"This way!" she yelled.

They pursued their quarry like hunters' hounds, but when they reached a crossroads, they couldn't be sure which tunnel the Mason had taken.

"We can't lose him now," said Edgar. "We're so close."

"Horace, you are still no help!" Ellen cried to the gargoyle who looked down on them silently.

Skreeee-KLANG!

"The manhole again!" Ellen shouted.

They reached the ladder nearest them. The manhole loomed far above. "Quickly, Ellen! We can still catch him above ground!" said Edgar.

He began to climb, but Ellen paused before following her brother.

"I wonder if he went *up* at all," she said. "Look."

Directly beneath her feet, a steel cover read "MAINTENANCE." These outlets were scattered throughout the sewers and led down to storage rooms beneath the main level. The twins had explored most of them, but never found anything of interest beyond a few rusty tools.

On this one, however, was a glob of odorous, white gunk.

"The telltale mark," said Ellen, crouching. She grabbed the heavy disk and gave it a heave. It opened with a horrid screech, revealing a narrow duct with iron rungs leading down. An orange light glowed below.

"Trapped like Pet in a drainpipe," said Edgar.

The twins descended the iron rungs and dropped onto a plush rug.

"What *is* this place?" whispered Edgar.

Rather than the dank, dirty closet they expected, the room could have been the fanciest parlour of the most elegant home in Nod's Limbs.

Oil lanterns cast flickering light on the stone, and a fire blazed in a cast-iron furnace. Paintings and maps decorated the walls. A high-backed armchair, ottoman, and side table sat in the middle of the room. Shelves displayed thick, leather-bound books and a variety of antique hand tools. But there was no Mason.

"We explored all of these maintenance rooms at one time or another — why didn't we ever see this?" said Ellen.

"Looks like things have changed since our last visit," said Edgar. He plucked a tool from a shelf; it boasted a twisted handle and a nasty double-pointed tip. "Look at this beauty. What on earth *is* it?"

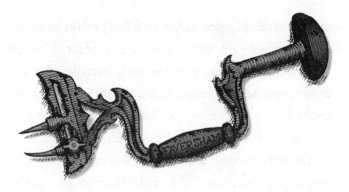

"That's a 1912 Faversham gasket cutter," said a voice behind them. "And there are only twenty left in the world."

34. Welcome to My Parlour

The twins whirled around to see a slim, hooded figure emerge from behind a tapestry.

Whatever the twins expected from the stranger, it was not the light, sweet laugh that greeted them. The Mason stepped forward and drew back the hood: a young woman stood before them.

She had sharp features – an angular nose and chin and thin cheeks. Fair hair fell over her shoulders, and her green eyes flashed in the dim light. She could not have been more than twenty. Atop her head sat strange black goggles, large and bulky, like a scuba diver's mask.

"Welcome to my private hideaway," she said, motioning about. "It is a long-abandoned family retreat. I recently restored this place to its former glory." She removed the goggles from her head.

"Ah, night vision," said Edgar. "Nice trick."

"You *are* observant," she said. "Except, of course, that you didn't see that hidden door in your own basement."

"We found you, didn't we?" said Ellen. "We're here to take back our things, you thief."

"So you really think you discovered me by your own detective skills, do you?" asked the Mason, laughing again. "I should hope you found me! I certainly made enough noise. A deaf rat could have followed that racket. No, I led you here. I made sure you saw me running away, and I left that gooey white mark on the maintenance hatch. Oh, yes," she pointed at Ellen, "and I also saved *you* from a nasty swim." Ellen clenched her fists.

"Lies! You're covering your blunder!" said Ellen. "The Mason charade is over. The underground is *our* domain."

Suddenly, the woman's amused expression disappeared. "My family built every inch of this sewer, laid every stone, and dug every channel!" she bellowed with the force of a wrecking ball. "This is *my* domain, little girl."

Edgar slipped his hand into his satchel and quietly switched on the tape recorder.

"Who *are* you?" he asked.

"I am the Mason."

"Waaait," said Ellen. "Your family built this place? Your name is on every capstone at every archway. You're a Smithy!"

The woman blinked. "Well done. I *am* a Smithy — Eugenia Smithy — and I'm the proud product of generations of engineering greatness."

"Say that you *did* lure us here. Why go to the trouble?" asked Edgar.

"I have a proposition for you," said the Mason. "How would you like to get rid of Smelterburg Construction once and for all?"

35. Great Minds Think Alike

"What do you mean?" asked Edgar.

"Sit and I shall explain everything." Eugenia moved to the armchair and gestured for the twins to share the ottoman.

"I don't like this, Edgar," whispered Ellen. "We should get our plans and get out of here."

"Let's see what she has to say," murmured Edgar. "Keep her talking." He patted the satchel softly and Ellen nodded. They took their places on the padded footrest.

"I'm glad to finally meet you," said Eugenia. "You do impressive work, as I first noticed at the French Toast Festival. Smithy & Sons had a photographer there to capture our giant syrup pitcher in action. When I studied the pictures of the disaster, I spied you striped gremlins in the middle of the mayhem."

The twins smiled in spite of themselves.

"Then I heard you scraping that dreadful car hood over the entrance to my little getaway. You moved an awful lot of bricks that night."

"So did you," said Ellen. "You stole our bricks and our plans. Why? What do you want with the junkyard?"

"I couldn't care less about the junkyard. I stand against the careless, shoddy Smelterburg Construction Corporation." Eugenia leaned forward in her chair.

"That Knightlorian contract should have gone to me, to my company. Smithy & Sons have built every important structure in Nod's Limbs since the founding of the town – Town Hall, the clock tower, homes, schools, businesses. For ten generations, the Smithy legacy brought strength *and* artistry to Nod's Limbs. The mayor's hotel is the biggest project in years, but he hired Smelterburg oafs with poor skills, even poorer standards, and absolutely no eye for *beauty*."

"So you're jealous," said Ellen.

Eugenia leaped from the chair. "I'll never be jealous of those artless, corner-cutting bunglers!" she cried. "They represent the opposite of everything Smithy & Sons stands for."

"I see," Ellen nodded. "Jealous."

"No, you don't understand. They... they... " Eugenia turned bright red and struggled to catch her breath. "They cost me the job I was born to have."

She composed herself and continued.

"When my father retired, I became the first woman to run Smithy & Sons – by age nineteen, no less! They were going to rename the company 'Smithy & Sons &

Daughter.' But then that snake Knightleigh chose Smelterburg for his dream project. He said Smelterburg would bring a 'brave new look to our town,' but I know he hired them because they were faster and cheaper. Well, maybe so, but you always get what you pay for. That idiot Gus didn't follow even the most basic rules of construction.

"When my father heard that we lost the project, he accused me of embarrassing the family and cast me from the company. But if I can drive Smelterburg out, Smithy & Sons may yet complete the hotel. And my father will give me my job back."

"Fired by Daddy," said Ellen. "Ouch."

"What does this have to do with us?" asked Edgar.

"I had plans to get rid of the Smelterburg crew, but they were too involved, too complicated. When I saw your plans for the bricks, I knew they were just the thing. Easy. Simple. You exhibited the kind of fresh thinking I needed."

"Simple? You thought our plans were simple?" asked Edgar. "Even the catapult?"

"Of course. I'm a builder's daughter."

"You can't think for yourself!" cried Ellen. "You're not an engineer, you're a thief!"

"I can improve any plan," said Eugenia. "I can see

the flaws and fix them. You designed Operation: Whiplash to blow down skaters at the ice rink – pointless child's play. I modified it with confetti, and look at the results!"

"I'll admit it *was* a dramatic flourish," said Edgar.

"Edgar!" Ellen kicked her brother's foot, but he ignored her.

"So, what are you planning to do with that balm? Gum up the gears of the bulldozers?"

"Balm? What are you talking about?" asked Eugenia.

"The white gunk in your lab – under our house," said Edgar.

"Heavens, that's not *my* lab!"

36. A Plotter's Demand

"Don't play dumb," said Ellen. "We know you're trying to protect that lab from being discovered. We read your journal."

"What journal?" Eugenia asked.

Ellen reached into Edgar's satchel for the diary, wrenching it from under Pet, whose hair seemed to hug the book. She flipped to a page and began to read:

> *The path of my day's walk nearly crossed that of K——'s, who would enjoy any chance to disgrace me. I resolve to concentrate more resolutely on my plans for the balm – no more venturing outside! If I can link my laboratory to the sewer I may yet move about town undetected.*

Ellen shut the book. "This *has* to be you!" she said. "'K' – Knightleigh, obviously. And all that sneaking about—"

"All I can tell you is that neither that book nor the laboratory is mine," said Eugenia. "I never saw the place until a few days ago. The night you moved the bricks, I noticed the mossy wall in your remote little arm of the sewer. That wall was not built by a Smithy. It was, of course, the secret door leading to the laboratory."

"Then whose lab is it?"

"I haven't any idea. Maybe the person who built your house."

Edgar and Ellen glanced at each other.

"But that is not our concern at the moment," Eugenia went on. "The plans I have of yours are not enough − delaying the crew will only work for so long. I want you to devise a way to drive the Smelterburg Construction Corporation out of Nod's Limbs for good."

Ellen turned to her brother. "Edgar, she is a nutcase."

"Clearly the both of you like causing public mayhem. This is your big chance. I can help you. Together, we can make an even bigger display than the French Toast Festival. You can cause Mayor Knightleigh untold grief, and I'll get my contract." Eugenia rose and paced the small room, twirling her goggles.

"And if we say no?" asked Ellen.

Eugenia stopped and faced them. Suddenly, the iron rungs of the entrance ladder sank noiselessly into the wall.

The twins were going nowhere.

37. As the Table Turns

"I was hoping we could enter a partnership," said Eugenia. "I did not want to have to use force."

Edgar examined the wall. "How did you do that?" he asked.

"What's more," Eugenia continued, "your precious plans are at stake." She took a tube of rolled papers from a cabinet and held them near the furnace. "Help me — or your designs will turn to ashes."

It was Eugenia's turn to be surprised as Ellen erupted in laughter.

"That's your threat? Go ahead, burn them!" cried Ellen.

Edgar choked. "Are you mad?"

"Edgar, if she burns them, she's through. She's out of ideas and her career as the Mason is over. But with our genius, dear brother, we can always—"

"We can always draw up more plans!" howled Edgar. "Feeble threats, you worthless bully! Better that our designs are ashes than in the wrong hands."

For the first time, Eugenia did not have an answer. Her eyes darted from twin to twin, but neither of her young guests showed signs of concern. Ellen picked up a few coals and tossed them in the fire, while Edgar went back to examining the wall where the iron rungs had been. "Ha! You dare to call my bluff?" Eugenia cried. She threw the rolled papers into the fire. The flame blazed and crackled.

"Interesting," said Edgar, still poking at the wall. "The mechanism is so well concealed that I can't disable it."

"You will help me, or else... or else..." Eugenia's eyes fell on Edgar's satchel and the small tuft of fur that stuck out of it. Before either twin could react, she leaped toward the bag. She grabbed Pet's scruff and yanked it out.

"Help me, or you'll never see your kitty here again!"

"Kitty?" asked Edgar and Ellen in unison.

"What do you say? Are you ready to bid farewell to Fluffy? It would be unfortunate if... if..."

For the first time, Eugenia looked carefully at the animal she held and realized that it was not, in fact, a kitty.

Or a hamster.

Or any other kind of creature she'd ever seen before.

Pet blinked its single eye, and Eugenia screamed and dropped it.

"What is that thing?" she shrieked. Having no other weapon at hand, she lamely threw her goggles at the hairy bundle. The goggles landed next to Pet, and then a grinding, metallic noise drew the twins' attention to the entranceway. The ladder rungs reappeared.

Edgar bent to pick up the goggles and gasped.

"A transmitter!" He showed his sister a button beneath the goggles' lens. "Genius." He pushed the button several times, watching the rungs surface and submerge into the stone. Finally, Ellen grabbed the goggles from him and took the tape recorder from his satchel. She turned to Eugenia.

"We have every word of your story on tape. If we see one more wayward brick, we'll tell the whole town who you are, and you won't get work as a ditch digger in Smelterburg. Let's go, Edgar. We're done here."

"Not quite," said Edgar, and he swiped the Faversham gasket cutter from its shelf.

The twins climbed out of the hideaway, leaving Eugenia stunned and silent by her roaring fire.

38. View from the Top

When they reached the top of the ladder, Edgar poked Ellen.

"Sister, we do have something in common with Eugenia," he said. "We want Smelterburg gone too."

"No, Brother, we don't," Ellen replied. "Smithy & Sons would just step in behind them. Same problem, different intruder."

The twins slipped through the cask door and climbed flight after flight of stairs to the top of the house, where they scaled one last ladder to the attic-above-the-attic. Edgar squinted through the eyepiece of their telescope to assess the bee situation below.

But he did not see a swarm of bees. He saw a swarm of men in hardhats. "Ellen! Knightleigh got rid of the bees! The Smelterburg workers are back to clear out the junkyard!"

"What? How did he—? Let me see!" Ellen pushed Edgar out of the way. Several workmen mingled about, not swatting at insects, but removing the last pieces of junk from the area. Suddenly, a gleaming vehicle whisked up to the cemetery entrance. It was the mayor's limousine.

"Great. Knightleigh's there too," said Ellen. It was not just the mayor, however. Stephanie, her little brother Miles, and their mother all piled out of the car, dressed in their finest. A man with a camera dangling

from his neck approached the family and led them into the junkyard.

"Hmph. A photo of the hotel groundbreaking for the newspaper," said Ellen. "I wish someone would break *them*."

Two workmen, meanwhile, wandered over to the corner of the junkyard. They briefly surveyed the grounds, then seized the nearest object. Ellen watched in horror as each man grabbed an end of Berenice's bed frame and heaved it onto their shoulders, ripping the plant from the ground.

Ellen shrieked and barrelled down the ladder.

Before Edgar followed, he turned back to the telescope, knowing and fearing what he would see.

Berenice's main stem was bent double, and most of her vines and tendrils were torn away. Her head lay in the dirt, miraculously still attached to the stem, but a gash reached from her lip to her gullet, and a dark, purplish liquid oozed from the wound.

The Knightleighs approached the spot with brand new shovels in hand, and they posed in a semicircle around the plant. The photographer knelt and pointed his camera at the family as Stephanie aimed her shovel at the broken body of Berenice and smiled.

"No," breathed Edgar, as he plunged down the stairs after his sister.

39. The Burial

"AAAAAAAIIIIIIIEEEEEEEE!"

Edgar heard the wail as he ran out the front door, and he knew he was too late. The sound, the vicious shriek of a banshee, echoed across the Gadget Graveyard. He found Ellen just inside the junkyard wall, barely hidden from the Knightleighs by the last of the trash heaps. She was staring at Stephanie.

The mayor's daughter held aloft the bedraggled remains of Berenice, whose severed roots hung off the edge of the shovel. The whole Knightleigh family seemed jolted by the scream, and they looked around to find the source. Edgar pulled Ellen behind a stack of steel girders.

"And, of course, cleaning out this junkyard will end the stray cat problem in the area," Mayor Knightleigh said. "Another positive contribution to the community from the Knightlorian Hotel."

"Yes, of course," said the photographer uneasily. "At any rate, I think we got the picture. We're done here."

"Ugh. Disgusting, mangy cats," said Stephanie. "And what kind of a horrible plant is this?" she asked, looking at the fallen form hanging on her shovel.

"A cool one," said Miles. "Why did you have to kill it, Steph? I wanted to keep it."

"Gross, Miles," Stephanie said. "Everything here is ugly. I want to go home."

"Hurry, into the car, dear. I can already feel the dirt underneath my fingernails," said their mother.

The Knightleighs laid down their shovels, returned to their limo, and rode off. The construction team packed up as well. Soon all was quiet, and Edgar emerged from his hiding place.

"Is it very bad?" Ellen asked quietly.

Edgar looked at Stephanie's abandoned shovel and Berenice. Her brown roots were shredded, and now her head was torn almost in two. The purplish fluid leaking from her fractured mouth had, here and there, dried to a crusty maroon.

"Yes. It is very bad," said Edgar.

Ellen approached slowly. She did not speak. Edgar looked at her warily. Normally, his sister was far from quiet when she was upset. Her stillness frightened him.

"Ellen?" he asked.

She was silent.

"Are you okay?"

Ellen didn't take her eyes off Berenice. She felt a prickly sensation in the base of her skull and a burning in her eyes. Her throat throbbed as if she had swallowed a rock.

"I think I might be getting sick," she said.

Edgar fidgeted. He tenderly yanked one of Ellen's pigtails, but Ellen still didn't respond.

"Let's scrounge around in the Gadget Graveyard before they cart the last of this stuff away," said Edgar. "I think I saw an industrial magnet by the wall."

Nothing.

He grabbed her hand. "Come on, Sister." He thought for a moment. "Hey, I have a great idea for a new game with Pet. It's called 'See Pet Bounce.'"

"Are you completely heartless? We can't just leave her here!" shrieked Ellen.

"What are we going to do with her? She's gone, Ellen – torn to pieces."

Ellen looked around wildly. Her eyes fell upon a nearby grassy area at the back of the neighboring cemetery.

"We'll bury her," she said. She picked up Berenice and a shovel and strode to the plot of grass. Edgar followed with another of the shovels.

Ellen carefully laid Berenice on the ground and began to dig. Edgar dug as well. Soon they had a small hole.

"Well, that's probably good enough," said Edgar.

"Six feet, Edgar! Everyone else here got six feet!" Ellen yelled, jabbing her brother with her shovel. "Keep digging!"

Edgar dared not disobey – her shovel was sharper than his. They continued until Ellen finally deemed the grave deep enough. She was about to lower

Berenice into it when Edgar pulled a handkerchief from his satchel.

"Here," he said. "A burial shroud."

Ellen wrapped the withered corpse in the hanky and gently placed Berenice at the bottom of the grave. "To dust," she whispered. She climbed out of the hole and began shovelling dirt back into it. When the grave was filled, the twins stood back.

"Wait! Wait just a second, Ellen," said Edgar suddenly, and he scrambled off to the junkyard. Ellen wandered back into the Gadget Graveyard as well, to the scene of the slaughter.

The hard, white seeds that once grew in Berenice's mouth were scattered over the ground: they had all fallen out at the swipe of Stephanie's cruel shovel. Some were stained from the plant's dark digestive juices, as if Berenice had coughed and sputtered blood.

Despite her failures in the past, Ellen vowed a final attempt to sprout one. She gathered every last seed and felt a twinge of hope.

Edgar ran up to her. "Here," he said, "a proper headstone." He handed Ellen a piece of broken cinderblock on which he had crudely carved "BERENICE" with the chisel from his satchel. They returned to the grave and placed the cinderblock at its head.

"I guess that's it," said Ellen. But before they left, a sad dirge poured forth, the last song for Berenice:

> 'Neath the bed frame, only dust knew
> How you sprouted, in the rust grew—
> Back to earth we now entrust you
> Where, as aught, you came before.
> Not to feed you insects gladly,
> Fair Berenice, we'll miss you madly,
> Here we leave you, sadly, sadly,
> Evermore and evermore.

40. The Fall of Edgar and Ellen

As they finished, Ellen gave one last pat to the earth with her shovel. Her whole body shook.

"I *must* be sick," she said, trying to steady her arm. "Look, I can't stop trembling."

"It's not just you, Sister," said Edgar. He, too, wobbled. "It's the ground! It's an earthquake!"

But it was not an earthquake. The twins heard a rumbling from below, and the ground gave way

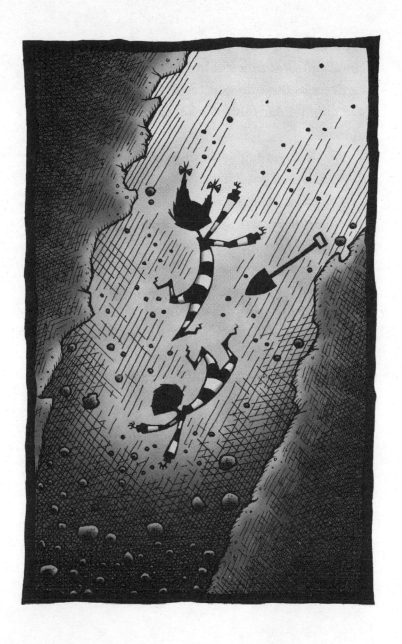

beneath them. They were falling – falling through a cloud of dirt into a sinkhole. Clumps of crumbling earth broke their tumble.

"Ugh!" Edgar pulled his head from under a clod of mud.

"Blech!" said Ellen, spitting dirt from her mouth. "Where are we?"

The twins looked around and saw a natural tunnel stretching away from them on either side.

"Not another hidden passage!" cried Edgar.

"This is a better resting place for Berenice anyway," said Ellen. "I don't want any of her murderers to see her grave."

Edgar furrowed his brows. He glanced up and down the corridor. Despite the darkness around them, the echoes of their voices indicated that the passage-way stretched far in both directions.

"Ellen, remember that honeycomb of caves that led up to Heimertz's shed?" he asked.

Ellen didn't answer. She sat, picking dirt out of her ear.

"That diary mentioned it too," Edgar continued. "These tunnels must form quite a network under the cemetery and the Gadget Graveyard."

"Would you stop talking about tunnels?" said Ellen. "They've been nothing but a nuisance. I can't believe it's so easy to fall through—"

Ellen stopped and stroked a pigtail.

"I see," she said. "They're building the hotel on top of Swiss cheese."

"I have an idea, Sister, but we may have to consult someone who knows transmitters."

41. Eugenia Balks

"I'm positive those caves you found run underneath the site," said Eugenia. "It's pure luck they haven't broken through already."

The twins had brought her to the Gadget Graveyard to explain their plan. The workmen had removed the last of the junk and started digging the giant pit where they would pour the concrete. Eugenia gazed over the side.

"The Smelterburg crew didn't survey the land at all," she said. "I can't stand sloppy work." She sighed.

"Fantastic. So we all get what we want then?" asked Edgar.

Eugenia stepped back from the foundation pit. "Your idea sounds dangerous," she said. "I don't want anything *demolished*. I build things. I don't destroy them."

"You just don't want to get your hands dirty," said Ellen.

"No, I won't do it," said Eugenia. "You'll have to think of something else."

Edgar removed the tape recorder from his satchel and switched it on.

"Remember this?" he asked as Eugenia's voice sounded through the speaker: *"Help me uproot the Smelterburg crew..."*

Edgar clicked off the tape and rewound it. "One misstep and we tell Knightleigh who the Mason really is."

"But if the whole site collapses—" Eugenia began.

"No one will get hurt, Eugenia, if that's what you're worried about," Edgar interrupted. "The area will be clear at that point."

"Smithy & Sons can still build the hotel," said Ellen. "You'll just have to suggest a new location."

42. Seedy Business

While Edgar and Eugenia stayed to take measurements in the Gadget Graveyard, Ellen retreated to the house to plant Berenice's seeds. On a table piled high with soil, pointy white seeds sat in a row in front of several pots.

"Berenice may be lost, but you, little ones, you're going to grow even bigger and hungrier," she said to the seeds as she nestled them in beds of dirt and sprinkled water on top. "I know this climate isn't your favourite, but I'll make sure you get plenty to eat. Perhaps all of you can feast on Stephanie." She patted down the topsoil in the last pot with a rusty spade and noticed that one seed remained.

"Hmmm. One more pot," Ellen said. She ran to the front hall where Edgar's satchel sat on its table. Inside she found one of the smelly beakers Edgar had taken from the laboratory. She did her best to clean it off.

"All this gunk—but you're the only container at hand," she said. She returned to her pots to plant the last seed.

43. Foundation Day

The big day finally arrived, and all of Nod's Limbs turned out for the event. Picnickers cautiously gazed over the edge of the great foundation pit before settling down on their blankets or lining up at the red-and-yellow striped tents selling hamburgers and hot dogs (which, for the occasion, had been renamed "Smelterburgers" and "Hot Digs"). Children emerged from the face-painting booth with images of hammers and nails on their cheeks, and they crowded the back of the lot, where Fire Chief Lugwood supervised bulldozer hayrides.

Mayor Knightleigh paced a makeshift stage that had been erected at the edge of the pit. A guard stood on either end.

"Don't worry, Daddy," said Stephanie as she joined her father. "The Mason can't do anything today – he wouldn't dare."

"Of course he wouldn't. I am the mayor, and I am here!" he said. But then he wiped a hand over his brow where sweat had begun to bead and leaned in close to Stephanie. "All the same," he whispered, "I want you to patrol the crowd. Keep an eye out for anything unusual."

"But I want to stand up here with you when you tell everyone the big news. I'm wearing my new outfit!" She pointed to her pleated lavender skirt.

"Listen to me, young lady. It is your duty to help today come off flawlessly. This hotel will bring fame and fortune to our family. Now do your part."

"Yes, Daddy," said Stephanie glumly. She stepped off the stage and into the mass of picnickers.

44. Drama Behind the Port-a-Loos

Edgar and Ellen peered out from behind a row of portable toilets. It was the most likely place to avoid the crowd, since most Nod's Limbsians refused anything but the lemony scents and quiet comfort of their well-kept lavatories at home.

Beside them, Eugenia Smithy nervously fingered a thin, flat metal box with a red button in the middle — a remote transmitter.

"Can we just get this over with?" she asked.

"No!" said the twins.

"Knightleigh is going to give his usual long-winded speech," said Ellen. "Then, at his moment of triumph — BAM! *That's* the proper time."

"Where's your sense of flair, Eugenia?" asked Edgar. "Our operation must have drama."

He eyed the cement trucks, whose enormous conical barrels rotated endlessly. Their chutes were poised over the empty pit, ready to deliver the payload when Mayor Knightleigh gave his signal.

"We just need to lie low for another hour or so," said Edgar.

"Everything you do is *low*," said a voice behind them.

All three conspirators spun around to see Stephanie Knightleigh.

"I thought I might find you here today," she said.

"You were *thinking?*" said Edgar. "Stephanie, you must be exhausted."

"Not nearly as tired as you, I'm sure, with all the trouble you've caused around town," she said. "Just wait until I tell my father I cornered the Mason. Or should I say, *Masons.*"

Ellen hunched her shoulders and clenched her fists. Her eyes were slits.

"Murderer," she snarled.

"What?" asked Stephanie.

"Murderer," Ellen growled again.

"What are you talking about? Have you lost your mind? I knew it would happen someday, but—"

Ellen came hurtling toward her. Stephanie leaped aside just in time.

"You're crazy!" Stephanie yelled. "I'm calling Daddy's guards." She ran off.

Ellen started to follow, but Edgar pulled her back.

"Don't be rash, Sister," he said. "There are rats and gasket cutters to use on her later. After Eugenia pushes the button, then you can – hey, where is Eugenia?"

The Mason was gone.

45. The Mayor's Bluff

Eugenia wandered through the cemetery, still fingering the remote. She stopped in front of a marble slab adorned with the images of a hammer and handsaw crossed like swords, and below them the words:

EZRA SMITHY

BUILD FOR JOY, DON'T DESTROY

It was her grandfather's grave; the epitaph was his personal philosophy, a credo she had grown up hearing and, until recently, lived by.

"I don't know what I'm doing. I'm sorry, Granddad," she said. "But I deserve this job – I mean, you would have done the same, wouldn't you?"

Her moment of reflection was interrupted by the sound of Mayor Knightleigh clearing his throat over the broadcast system.

> *"My fellow Nod's Limbsians, welcome to this historic day. Years from now, you can tell your children, grandchildren, and great-grandchildren that you were here to witness the beginning of a new age in Nod's Limbs!*
>
> *"But the pouring of the Knightlorian foundation is not the only momentous occasion on this day. I am proud to announce that through the tireless energy of me, my office, and the Nod's Limbs Police Department, we have apprehended the person who has so terrorised this fair town. Ladies and gentlemen, we have captured the Mason!"*

A wave of excitement rippled through the crowd. "Saints be praised! They caught him!"

"It was only a matter of time – NLPD is the finest police force you'll ever see!"

Edgar exchanged looks with Ellen.

"Who does the mayor think he's got?" he asked.

In the cemetery, Eugenia backed away from her grandfather's resting place.

"The Mason? He thinks he has the Mason?" she exclaimed. She looked about wildly, as if police officers with chains would leap from behind the headstones at any moment.

Mayor Knightleigh waved his hands to calm the crowd.

"To show you all that there is nothing left to fear, I brought the scoundrel here today. Now, now, I know this may be frightening for some of you, but all Nod's Limbsians must realize that this monster cannot harm us any longer!"

The crowd gasped again as Mayor Knightleigh walked to the edge of the stage, where a guard ushered a handcuffed young man up the stairs. He had long, unkempt hair and thick black glasses. His ratty beard hung a little crookedly from his chin.

"Mr Mayor, this wasn't in the description for my internship," the young man whispered to Mayor Knightleigh.

"Quiet, Bob. It falls under Clause 233: 'All interns must abide by and uphold the legitimacy of mayoral decrees by fulfilling any duty the mayor deems necessary,'" said the mayor.

"But how long do I have to stay in jail?"

"Just overnight. I must say, I'm a little disappointed in your attitude, Bob." The mayor steered Bob to the middle of the stage. A shudder flowed through the spectators.

"This is the man who began the nightmare, the fiend who scared us in our beds. But no more — I will ensure that he is tried and convicted to the full extent of my laws!"

Eugenia choked. "He arrested the wrong person!" she said. "The wrong person… could go to jail. An innocent man…" Knightleigh continued speaking, but she did not hear him. She looked from Ezra Smithy's grave to the remote control to the downtrodden man on the stage. "Build for joy…"

She dashed to the podium.

46. Confessions of a Guilty Anarchist

"Wait! Wait!" Eugenia shouted, ducking a guard and running up the stairs to Mayor Knightleigh.

"Ah, one of my many admirers. Your gratitude is most appreciated – oh, you're the Smithy girl. Young lady, I'm sorry your company is not building my hotel, but this is hardly the time—"

"You have the wrong person!" cried Eugenia. At the same moment Stephanie Knightleigh reached the stage and called, "That's not the Mason!" The microphone picked up their words, and their voices echoed across the picnic grounds.

"What?" Mayor Knightleigh laughed nervously. "Of course it is – just look at him. Guilty as sin. Plus, he confessed." He glared at his daughter. Stephanie tried to speak, but Eugenia cut in.

"It is *not* the Mason, I can assure you," she said. "All along, the Mason has been against one thing – the construction of this hotel. Blocking the bridge kept the trucks from getting here – so did the confetti storm. The bees made the site unworkable…"

The assembled townspeople stood silent, except for two pale figures in the back.

"I knew she'd lose her nerve," said Ellen.

"What is the first rule of planning the perfect scheme, Sister?"

"Trust no one, Brother."

"And the second?"

"Always have a backup plan."

Mayor Knightleigh tried to escort Eugenia from the stage.

"My dear girl, who would possibly want to sabotage this hotel? It will mean great things for me – I mean, for Nod's Limbs!"

"I have proof – a taped confession of the *real* Mason. And the Mason is… the Mason is—"

But just then, in the distance, Eugenia heard a *twanggg.*

47. How to Build a Very Tall Building

The key to any structure's strength lies in its foundation. This is the pit that construction teams fill with cement to support the building with something stronger than plain dirt. When people sleep or eat or throw housewarming parties, they rest easy knowing that their walls stand firm upon rock-hard concrete.

When constructing a really tall hotel – say, eleven storeys high – the builders need a much deeper hole in very solid earth (not, for example, earth with lots of tunnels through it). They want that cement to provide an unmovable footing so the structure doesn't tip or topple. Although the Leaning Tower of Pisa makes a marvellous postcard, it would make a terrible hotel. All the guests would complain of lipsticks rolling off their counters and room service carts careening into walls.

That's why, on Knightlorian Foundation Day, one large mixing truck was backed up to each side of the pit. Four trucks waited to pour tons of sloshing, gurgling, messy cement into the hole at the proper moment.

What a useful tool for fiendish minds.

48. The Flight of the Bowling Ball

 *Twanggg!* went the catapult, launching a bowling ball high over the trees and straight toward the Gadget Grave-yard. It plunged into a red wheelbarrow.

Bull's-eye!

The ball flipped the wheelbarrow in a spectacular somersault. A fishing line tied to the wheelbarrow's handle yanked the pull cord of a lawn mower engine, which chugged to life.

"No, no, no," whispered Eugenia as she stood watching helplessly from the podium. "I didn't press the button."

But the lawn mower plugged away nevertheless, doing exactly what she designed it to do. A shaft on the engine spun madly, reeling in a slim string that passed under every mixing truck perched at the edge of the foundation pit. Only a very ingenious, mechanically minded person could have rigged that string to do what it now did.

All at once, each truck shifted from PARK to REVERSE. A cacophony of *beep-beep-beep*s filled the air as the trucks warned the world they were moving backward. Their engines roared as if someone pushed their gas pedals flat to the floor, and then, like four synchronized swimmers plunging together, the trucks surged into the air. They met directly over the centre of the pit, creating an explosion of twisted metal, shattered glass, and wet concrete.

This mass landed with an impact that shook the ground far beyond the borders of Nod's Limbs, and the flimsy layer of dirt at the bottom of the hole gave way.

With a mighty splash, concrete and metal gushed into the tunnels below. A tower of dust rose from the pit, and bits of dirt and rock rained down. Fragments of mangled trucks sank into the spilled cement, slowly muffling the last of the *beep*s until all was silent.

49. Bob Has a Theory

"My hotel – my beautiful, wonderful, perfect hotel! Now it can never be built!" Mayor Knightleigh shook his head in his hands, then turned furiously to Eugenia.

"You know who the Mason is? *Who? Tell me! I'll squash him like... like...*"

"A grape, sir?" suggested Bob the intern.

"Quiet, Bob," said the mayor. "A grape! *I'll squash him like a grape!*"

Eugenia stood speechless. All she could mutter was, "Those twins... those twins..."

"What about twins? I don't care about twins. Who is the Mason?" Knightleigh demanded.

"The twins – I knew it!" said Stephanie.

Bob removed his fake beard and peeked over the edge of the pit, along with many in the crowd. Below them, they saw that even the largest chunks of wreckage had sunk to the depths of the concrete pool, leaving a surface as smooth and calm as a lake on a windless night.

"You know, Mr Mayor," called Bob. "I think there must have been a massive cavern beneath the pit."

The mayor glowered at his young intern. "What? What has that got to do with this disaster?"

"Sir, if you had built the hotel here, it would have eventually collapsed!" Bob's voice rang out over the speakers, and a concerned murmur rippled through the picnic grounds.

"Now, Bob – *ahem* – stop alarming the good citizens," said the mayor in his most reassuring voice as he glanced at the audience. "We have the world-class skills of Smelterburg Construction Corporation working for us. Certainly they would have known if this were unstable ground."

"Certainly," said Bob. "So why didn't they tell you it might collapse so easily?"

Mayor Knightleigh watched a number of heads in the crowd begin to nod. A few scattered voices piped up:

"That scruffy young man is right! Why didn't they tell us this could happen?"

"Indeed, this smacks of sabotage!"

The mayor stepped quickly to the microphone and seized it. "Smelterburg! Yes, I see it now! I knew Mayor Blodgett was planning a competing tourism initiative, but I never imagined he'd take it this far. He sent his criminal construction crew to our fair town to sabotage my new – er, *our* new hotel. And at a public ceremony so we'd all look like fools! Then they sacrificed their trucks to throw us off the track. *Smelterburg is the Mason!* Isn't that right, Miss Smithy? Isn't that what you were going to tell me?"

Eugenia did not respond at first. She stared at the mayor for several seconds, then slowly nodded her head.

Mayor Knightleigh raised his hands and turned to the picnickers. "Let us be thankful, fellow citizens, that the Special Mayoral Investigative Unit uncovered Smelterburg's dastardly plan that would have cost us countless dollars – and perhaps lives."

The crowd recoiled with cries of shock. Mayor Knightleigh continued.

"Oh, yes, lives! Good job, Agent Bob. This man's undercover work as a *decoy* Mason was all part of my plan to draw out the *real* Mason.

"Now, citizens, I assure you that the Knightlorian Hotel will yet rise to the skies! We will find another site and begin anew—"

In a sea of glum faces, two broad grins bobbed happily. Edgar and Ellen elbowed their way to the front. They were slightly out of breath, having run all the way from their catapult in the Black Tree Forest Preserve.

"No, Mr Mayor, we won't need a new site," said Eugenia, who peered into the cavity.

It was the mayor's turn to stare. "What do you mean?"

"It appears to me that the concrete has completely filled the tunnels below the surface," she said. "The foundation for the Knightlorian will be stronger than ever. You *can* build your hotel here."

"What?" exclaimed the mayor and the twins as one.

Edgar and Ellen stepped onto the stage.

"Eugenia, you traitorous snake," said Ellen.

"I give as good as I get," Eugenia replied.

"See, the children of the community are so overwhelmed with joy that they rush to the stage," Mayor Knightleigh said. "Yes, share your civic spirit with all of us!"

"Here's something to overwhelm you – proof of the *real* Mason," said Edgar as he pulled his tape recorder from his satchel and held it in front of the microphone. "Listen to this!"

Eugenia dived for Edgar, but he had already pushed the play button.

"I can't wait to finish the job and get back to Smelterburg. The way we're going, this hotel is doomed." The voice of Gus, the Smelterburg Construction Corporation foreman, boomed from the loudspeakers.

50. A League of Enemies

"Edgar! That's the wrong part of the tape."

"I know. I don't understand. I must have rewound too far!"

"You dunce! Eugenia—"

"Eugenia is very thankful to her dear friends for their excellent detective work," said Eugenia, snatching the tape recorder from Edgar. "Mr Mayor, as I said, your hotel can proceed as planned – well, with a few changes to the design. May I suggest, however, that you employ a more loyal and skilled firm than Smelterburg Construction?"

"Of course, Miss Smithy. My apologies for not consulting you first on the soundness of this site. The Smithys have built all the finest structures in Nod's Limbs." He turned to Gus, who was scrambling onto the stage. *"Smelterburg!"*

"Mr Mayor, I swear, this is a mistake! We were *delayed* by this Mason. We just wanted to do our jobs," said Gus. At least, this is what he *tried* to say. With a swollen, bee-stung tongue, he *sounded* much different: "Mitta Mayah, I dwear, dit id a midake—"

"Insensible blather? Why, he's been driven mad by guilt!" cried the mayor. "Guards, seize this Mason mastermind, this fraudulent foreman!"

As the mayoral guards dragged Gus away, Mayor Knightleigh gestured to Eugenia. "My dear, we have some plans to discuss."

"I'll be right there, Mr Mayor," Eugenia replied. She approached the twins.

"I'm sorry it turned out this way," she said. "But I am a builder, and I must follow my calling. I do thank you for all your help. The Mason would be proud of that bowling ball idea." She grinned and followed after the mayor.

"Turncoat," growled Ellen.

"We practically poured the foundation for them," said Edgar, "and now we can't stop this hotel. Blast Eugenia! She probably had this planned from the beginning."

The twins looked at each other and then at the retreating Mason.

"No," said Ellen. "That would have required imagination."

The twins shuffled home, heads hung low, singing a mournful tune:

To our sadness, to our sorrow,
No more scavenging tomorrow,
No more scrapped debris to borrow—

Mason fiend! Our cause of woe!
How did it ever come to this?
Our perfect plan should run amiss,
Berenice destroyed by shovel's kiss,
Our gadgets lost to the abyss?
Down underground our schemes are bound
Forever in this concrete drowned.

51. Shoot

31 August

Pilosoculus and I have returned from a lengthy tour of small towns along the coast. I took a few boxes of our finished product to see for myself how people would react to it—the results have pleased me beyond all measure! One morning in South Pineville, a frail old woman bounded into our inn and threw her arms around me. She had bought a box the night before, and she reported feeling the best she had in years. O joyous day! An odd note: Pilos seemed sluggish the entire trip and has only resumed its normal zest back in the lab. I suppose the dear creature only thrives on the substance in its pure form—I must remember not to leave it cut off from the laboratory for long.

"Pet! What are you doing? Get away from that book!" said Ellen as she entered the library.

Pet sat on the desk in front of the diary. Its eyeball had been focused on the pages of the journal, but it quickly looked up and attempted to sidle away before Ellen could reach it. She could swear that it tried to push the diary along as well.

"Pet, we need to have a long chat about this strange behavior of yours."

Ellen scooped up the creature and looked suspiciously from it to the diary and back again.

"Ha! As if *you* could read," she said, slamming the book shut and tucking Pet under her arm. "Come on, Pet, it's time to play a new game. Edgar calls it 'See Pet Bounce.'"

As she left the room, she glanced at the window, where a row of jars lined the sill.

"Still no growth," she sighed.

But at the end of the window sill, partly concealed by the tattered curtain, sat the beaker, its glass a bit smeared.

A green shoot poked through the dirt, basking in the fading sun.

THE END

Edgar & Ellen

PET'S REVENGE

WHOSE LAB HAVE the twins discovered? What are the secrets of the old journal? And what has got into Pet? The mystery deepens as Pet fights back.

Coming Soon!

Edgar & Ellen

TOURIST TRAP

It's election season in Nod's Limbs, and Edgar and Ellen get wind of plans for an initiative to boost the local economy. The town's pending landmark status and the Mayor's own reputation depend on making Nod's Limbs a premier tourist destination. Edgar and Ellen will make sure the goody-goody Mayor and townspeople get all the attention they deserve!

www.EdgarAndEllen.com

Edgar & Ellen

High Wire

A BIZARRE CIRCUS APPEARS IN THE DEAD OF NIGHT, bringing caravans of strange entertainers to Nod's Limbs. The twins, however, find kindred spirits among the big top's fire-eaters and escape artists. Will Edgar and Ellen join up and leave Nod's Limbs to escape the wrath of Heimertz? What plans does the terrifying caretaker have for Pet? In a world of smoke and mirrors, is anything what it appears to be?

Coming Soon!